BACK
IN THE
WORLD

GRAVITY'S RAINBOW by Thomas Pynchon
THE HEADMASTER'S PAPERS by Richard A. Hawley
HOUSEKEEPING by Marilynne Robinson
HUNGER OF MEMORY by Richard Rodriguez
A JEST OF GOD by Margaret Laurence
JOHNNY GOT HIS GUN by Dalton Trumbo
LITTLE BIRDS by Anaïs Nin
LOVE MEDICINE by Louis Erdrich
A MEASURE OF TIME by Rosa Guy
ONE DAY IN THE LIFE OF IVAN DENISOVICH by Alexander I.
    Solzhenitsyn
THE RIVER WHY by David James Duncan
THE SNOW LEOPARD by Peter Matthiessen
SOPHIE'S CHOICE by William Styron
A SPY IN THE HOUSE OF LOVE by Anaïs Nin
THE STONE ANGEL by Margaret Laurence
SUNDOG by Jim Harrison
AN UNKNOWN WOMAN by Alice Koller
V. by Thomas Pynchon

BACK
IN THE
WORLD

STORIES BY

Tobias Wolff

BANTAM BOOKS

TORONTO · NEW YORK · LONDON · SYDNEY · AUCKLAND

This low-priced Bantam Book
contains the complete text of the
original hard-cover edition.
NOT ONE WORD HAS BEEN OMITTED.

BACK IN THE WORLD

A Bantam Book / published by arrangement with
Houghton Mifflin Company

PRINTING HISTORY
Houghton Mifflin edition published September 1985
Bantam edition / October 1986

The stories in this book originally appeared in the following magazines: Antaeus,
The Atlantic, Esquire, The Missouri Review, Ploughshares, TriQuarterly, and
Vanity Fair.

Windstone and accompanying logo of a stylized W are trademarks of Bantam Books, Inc.

Library of Congress Cataloging-in-Publication Data

Wolff, Tobias, 1945–
   Back in the world.

   Contents; Coming attractions—The missing person—
Say yes—[etc.]
   I. Title.
PS3573.0558B23   1986   813'.54   86-47560
ISBN 0-553-34325-4

Published simultaneously in the United States and Canada

PRINTED IN THE UNITED STATES OF AMERICA

O   0 9 8 7 6 5 4 3 2 1

for Rosemary
my mother

The author wishes to thank the
John Simon Guggenheim Memorial Foundation
for its generous support.

CONTENTS

COMING
ATTRACTIONS

Jean was alone in the theater. She had seen the customers out, locked the doors, and zipped up the night's receipts in the bank deposit bag. Now she was taking a last look around while she waited for her boss to come back and drive her home.

Mr. Munson had left after the first show to go ice skating at the new mall on Buena Vista. He'd been leaving early for almost a month now and at first Jean thought he was committing adultery against his wife, until she saw him on the ice one Saturday afternoon while she was out shoplifting with her girlfriend Kathy. They stopped by the curved window that ran around the rink and watched Mr. Munson crash into the wall several times. "Fat people shouldn't skate," Kathy said, and they walked on.

Most nights Mr. Munson came back to the theater around eleven. This was the latest he had ever been. It was almost twelve o'clock.

Someone had left an orange scarf on one of the seats in the back row. Under the same seat lay a partially eaten hambone and a bottle of hot sauce. The hambone still looked like what it was, an animal's leg, and when she saw it Jean felt weak. She picked up the scarf and left the food for Mr. Munson to deal with. If he said anything about it she would just play dumb. She put the scarf in the lost-and-found bag and walked toward the front of the theater, glancing from side to side to scan the lengths of the rows.

Halfway down the aisle Jean found a pair of sunglasses. They were Guccis. She dropped them in the bag and tried to forget about them, as if she were a regular honest person who did not steal lost items and everything else that wasn't bolted down, but Jean knew that she was going to keep the sunglasses and this knowledge made her resistance feel ridiculous. She walked a few rows farther, then gave a helpless shrug as if someone were watching and took the sunglasses out of the bag. They didn't fit. Her face was too narrow for them, her nose too thin. They made everything dim and kept slipping down, but Jean left them on as she worked her way toward the front of the theater.

In the first row on the right, near the wall, Jean saw a coat draped over one of the seats. She moved along the row to pick it up. Then she stopped and took off the sunglasses, because she had decided to believe that the coat was not a coat, but a dead woman wearing a coat. A dead woman all by herself in a theater at midnight.

Jean closed her eyes and made a soft whimpering noise like a dreaming dog makes. It sounded phony to her, so she stopped doing it; she opened her eyes and walked back along the row and up the aisle toward the lobby.

Jean put the lost-and-found bag away, then stood by the glass entrance doors and watched the traffic. She leaned forward as each new line of cars approached, looking through her own reflected face for Mr. Munson's Toyota. The glass grew so foggy from her breath that Jean could barely see through it. She became aware of her breathing, how shallow and fast it was. The game with the coat had scared her more than she'd meant it to. Jean watched some more cars go by. Finally she turned away and crossed the lobby to Mr. Munson's office.

Jean locked the office door behind her, but the closed door made her feel trapped. She unlocked the door again and left it open. From Mr. Munson's desk she could see the Coke machine and a row of posters advertising next week's movie. The desktop was empty except for the telephone and a picture of Mrs. Munson standing beside a snowdrift back where the Munsons used to live — Minnesota or Wisconsin. Mrs. Munson had on a parka, and she was pointing at the top of the drift to show how tall it was.

The snow made Jean think of her father.

It was quiet in the office. Jean laid her head on her crossed arms and closed her eyes. Almost at once she opened them again. She sat up and pulled the telephone across the desk and dialed her father's number. It was three hours later there and he was a heavy sleeper, so she let the phone ring for a long time. At first she held the receiver tight against her ear. Then she laid it down on the desk and listened to it until she heard a voice. Jean picked up the receiver again. It was her stepmother, Linda, saying "Hello? . . . Hello? . . . Hello? . . ." Jean would have hung up on her but she heard the fear in Linda's voice like an echo of her own, and she couldn't do it. "Hello," she said.

"Hello? Who is this, please?"

"Jean," Jean murmured.

"Gee-Gee? Is this Gee-Gee?"

"It's me," Jean said.

"It's you," Linda said. "My God, you gave me a fright."

"I'm sorry."

"What time is it out there?"

"Twelve. Ten past twelve."

"It's three o'clock in the morning here, lambchop. We're later than you are."

"I know."

"I just wondered if maybe you thought we were earlier. Wow, just hang on till I get myself together." A moment later Linda said, "There. Pulse normal. All systems go. So where are you, anyway?"

"At work."

"That's right, your dad told me you had a job. Gee-Gee with a job! You're just turning into a regular little grown-up, aren't you?"

"I guess," Jean said.

"Well, I think that's just super."

Jean nodded.

"I'm big on people doing for themselves," Linda said. "Fifteen isn't too young. I started work when I was twelve and I haven't stopped since."

"I know," Jean said.

Linda laughed. "Christ almighty, the jobs I've had. I could tell you stories."

Jean smiled politely into the receiver. She caught herself doing it and made a face.

"I guess you want to talk to old grumpy bear," Linda said.

"If that's okay."

"I hope it isn't bad news. You're not preggers, are you?"

"No."

"How about your brother?"

"Tucker isn't pregnant either," Jean said. "He hasn't started dating yet."

Linda laughed again. "I didn't mean *that*. I meant how *is* he?"

"Tucker's doing fine."

"And your mom?"

"She's fine too. We're all fine."

"That's great," Linda said, "because you know how your dad is about bad news. He's just not set up for it. He's more of a good news person."

Jean gave Linda the finger. She mashed it against the mouthpiece, then said, "Right." And Linda *was* right. Jean knew that, knew she wouldn't have said anything even if her father had come to the telephone except how great she was, and how great Tucker and her mom were, because telling him anything else would be against the rules. "Everyone's fine," Jean repeated. "I just had this urge to talk to him, that's all."

"Sure you did," Linda said. "Don't think he doesn't get the same urge sometimes."

"Tell him hi," Jean said. "Sorry I woke you up."

"That's what we're here for, dumpling. I'll see if I can get him to write you. He keeps meaning to, but letters are hard for him. He likes to be more hands-on with people. Still, I'll see what I can do, okay? You take care now."

Jean smashed the phone down and yelled "Fool!" She leaned violently back in the chair and crossed her legs. "Stupid hag," she said. "Vegetable."

She went on like this until she couldn't think of anything else. Then she called her mother's apartment. Tucker answered the phone. "Tucker, what are you doing up?" Jean asked.

"Nothing," Tucker said. "You're supposed to be home. Mom said you'd be home now."

"And you're supposed to be in bed," Jean told him. She heard a woman's voice shrieking, then two gunshots and a blare of music. "I can't believe you're still up," Jean said. "Let me speak to Mom."

"What?"

"Let me speak to Mom."

"She's not here," Tucker said. "Jean, know what?"

Jean closed her eyes.

"There's a bicycle in the swimming pool," Tucker said. "In the deep end. Under the diving board. Mrs. Fox told me I could keep it if we get it out. It's red," he added.

"Tucker, where's Mom? I want to talk to her."

"She went out with Uncle Nick."

"Where?"

Tucker didn't answer.

"Where did they go, Tucker?"

Tucker still didn't answer. Jean heard the sound of police sirens and squealing tires, and knew that he was watching the television again. He'd forgotten all about her. She screamed his name into the receiver. "What?" he said.

"Where are the grownups?"

"I don't know. Jean, are you coming home now?"

"In a few minutes. Go to bed, Tucker."

"Okay," he said. Then he said, "Bye," and hung up.

Jean got the telephone book out of the desk, but she could not remember Nick's last name. His number was probably lying around the apartment somewhere; in fact she knew it was, she had seen it, on her mom's bedside table or stuck to the refrigerator with a magnet. But if she asked Tucker to look for it he would get all confused and start crying.

Jean stood and went to the doorway. A jogger wearing phosphorescent stripes ran past the lobby window. The Coke machine gave a long rattling shudder, then went off with a sigh. Jean felt hungry. She got herself a package of Milk Duds from the refreshment counter and carried them back to Mr. Munson's office, where she chewed mouthful after mouthful until her jaws were tired. Jean put the rest of the Milk Duds in her purse with the sunglasses. Then she took out the telephone book and looked for the name of her English teacher, Mr. Hopkins. Mr. Hopkins also taught Driver's Ed and Kathy said that he had practically climbed on top of her when they were doing parallel parking. Jean hated him for that. How could someone recite poetry the way Mr. Hopkins did and still want Kathy?

His number wasn't in the book. Jean kept flipping through the pages. She chose a name and dialed the number and a man answered right away. In a soft voice he said, "Yes." Not "Yes?" but "Yes," as if he'd been expecting this call.

"Mr. Love," Jean said, "have I got news for you."

"Who is this?" he asked. "Do you know what time it is?"

"The news just came in. We thought you'd want to hear it right away. But if you wish to refuse the call all you have to do is say so."

"I'm not sure I understand," Mr. Love said.

"Do you wish to refuse the call, Mr. Love?"

He did not answer right away. Then he said, "Don't tell me I won something."

"Won something? Mr. Love, that is the understatement of the century."

"Just a minute," he said. "I have to get my glasses."

"This *is* Mr. Love, I assume," Jean asked when he returned to the telephone.

"Yes, ma'am. One and the same."

"We can't be too careful," Jean told him. "We're not talking about a bunch of steak knives here."

"I've never won anything before," Mr. Love said. "Just spelling bees. When I was a kid I could spell the paint off the walls."

"I guess I've got you on the edge of your seat," Jean said. Mr. Love laughed.

"You sound like a nice person," Jean said. "Where are you from?"

Mr. Love laughed again. "You're deliberately tying me up in knots."

Jean said, "We have a few standard questions we like to ask." She took the sunglasses from her purse and slipped them on. She leaned back and looked up at the ceiling. "We like to get acquainted with our winners."

"You've got me in a state," Mr. Love said. "All right, here goes. Born and raised in Detroit. Joined the navy after Pearl Harbor. Got my discharge papers in San Diego, June 'forty-six, and moved up here a couple weeks later. Been here ever since. That's about it."

"Good. So far so good. Age, Mr. Love?"

"Sixty-one."

"Marital status?"

"No status at all. I'm a single man."

"Do you mean to say, Mr. Love, that you have lived more than half a century and never entered into holy matrimony?"

Mr. Love was silent for a moment. Then he said, "Come on now — what's all this about?"

"One more question, Mr. Love. Then we'll talk prizes."

Mr. Love said nothing, but Jean could hear him breathe. She picked up the photograph of Mrs. Munson and laid it face down on the desk. "Here's the question, Mr. Love. I lie and steal and sleep around. What do you think about that?"

"Ah," Mr. Love said. "So I didn't win anything."

"Well, sir, no. I have to say no."

He cleared his throat and said, "I don't follow."

"It's a prank," Jean told him. "I'm a prankster."

"I understand that. I just don't see the point. What's the point?"

Jean let the question pass.

"Well, you're not the first to make a fool out of me," Mr. Love said, "and I suppose you won't be the last."

"I don't actually sleep around," Jean said.

He said, "You need to learn some concern for other people. Do you go to church?"

"No, sir. Sometimes back home we used to, but not here. Only once on Easter. The priest didn't even give a sermon. All he did was play a tape of a baby being born, with whale songs in the background." Jean waited for Mr. Love's reaction. He didn't seem to have one. "I don't actually sleep around," Jean repeated. "Just with one of my teachers. He's married," she added.

"Married!" Mr. Love said. "That's terrible. How old are you?"

"He thinks I'm brilliant," Jean said. "Brilliant and seductive. He kept staring at me in class. The next thing I knew he was writing poems on the back of my essays, and that's how it started. He's hopelessly in love with me but I could care less. I'm just playing him along."

"God in heaven," Mr. Love said.

"I'm awful to him. Absolutely heartless. I make fun of him in front of my friends. I do imitations of him. I even do imitations of him in bed, all the sounds he makes and everything. I guess you could say I'm just totally out of control. Don't ask me to tell you where it is, but I have this tattoo that says X-RATED. It's my motto. That and 'Live fast, die young.' Whenever I'm doing something really depraved I always say 'Live fast, die young.' I probably will, too."

"I'm at a loss," Mr. Love said. "I wish I knew what to do here."

He was quiet.

"Say something," Jean told him. "Bawl me out."

"I don't know you. I don't even know your name. I might be of some help if I knew your name."

"Fat chance," Jean said.

"Then I just don't know what to say."

Jean heard the snapping of the lock in the lobby door. "Adieu," she said, and hung up. She took the sunglasses off and put them in her purse, then stood and walked around the desk in time to see Mr. Munson swinging toward the office between a pair of crutches, one plaster-bound foot held cocked behind him. There was a bandage across his forehead. "Don't say a word," he told Jean. "I don't want to talk about it." Mr. Munson lurched past her into the office. "Just a little difficulty on the ice," he said bitterly. "Just a little taste of the old Munson karma." He took the bank deposit bag from the drawer where Jean kept it for him, unzipped it, leaned forward on the crutches, and shook the money onto the desktop. "Here," he said. Without looking up, Mr. Munson held out a five to Jean. "There's a cab waiting out front."

"A cab?"

"Do you expect me to drive in this condition? Look at me, for Christ's sake. I'm a mess."

"You don't look that bad," Jean told him.

"I look like the goddam *Spirit of 'Seventy-six* or something," Mr. Munson said. He lowered himself into the chair and propped his crutches against the desk. "I used to be good," he said, "I mean really good." He raised his eyes to Jean. "I'm nice to you, aren't I? I don't yell at you when you screw up. I don't say anything when you sneak your little friend in. You shouldn't look at me like that," he said. "You should try to look sorry."

Tucker was asleep on the floor in front of the television. Jean opened the Hide-a-Bed and managed to get him into his pajamas and between the covers without waking him up. Then she ransacked her mother's room for Nick's telephone number. She didn't find it, but she did find a new letter from her father. Jean sat on the bed and read the letter through, scowling at the sugary words he used, sometimes repeating them in a sarcastic tone. They still wrote each other love letters, her mother and father, but they had no right to; not now, not after what they'd done. It was disgusting.

Jean went to her own room. She read *Silas Marner* for a while, then got undressed and stood in front of the mirror. She studied herself. She turned and glanced coldly over her shoulder.

Jean faced the mirror again and practiced looking sad but brave. Then she got the sunglasses out of her purse and put them on, along with one of the blouses she'd stolen at Bullock's last weekend. She switched off all the lights except the swag lamp above her desk, so that she looked as if she were standing under a streetlight. The blouse hung halfway down her bare thighs. Jean turned the wide collar up, and lowered her eyelids, and let her mouth fall open a little. "I think of you all the time," she whispered, reciting her father's words, "every day and

every night, dearest love, only love of my life." Jean moved
her shoulders sinuously to make the sequins shimmer.
"Dearest sackbutt," she said. "Dearest raisinbrain." She
pursed her lips and made her eyelids flutter.

Tucker yelled something from the next room.

Jean went to the doorway. "Go to sleep, Tucker."

"I want Mom," Tucker said.

Jean took the sunglasses off. Tucker was sitting up in
bed, looking wildly around as if he didn't know where he
was. Jean walked across the room and sat down beside him.
"Mom'll be home in a minute." Tucker's hair was sticking up all over, and Jean began to smooth it down. "You
want a glass of water?"

"I want Mom."

"Listen, Tucker." Jean kept combing back his hair with
her fingers. "Listen, tomorrow is going to be a really
special day but it won't come unless you go to sleep."

He looked around the room again, then back at Jean.
"Special how?"

"You'll see."

"You mean when I wake up?"

"Right, but first you have to go to sleep." Jean pushed
against Tucker as she stroked his hair, and at last he re-
lented and lay down again.

"Promise?" he said.

"Promise."

When Tucker was asleep Jean got up and went outside.
She leaned against the door, her skin bristling with cold,
and looked around at the other apartments. All of them
were dark. Jean hugged herself and padded along the
rough wooden walkway, down the steps to the courtyard.

The pool lights were still on so that nobody would fall

in and sue. Still hugging herself, Jean tested the water
with one foot. It was icy. Mrs. Fox must have turned off
the heat. That was just like her, to turn the heat on in the
summer and turn it off in the winter. Stupid witch. It
wasn't even her money. Jean sniffed and rubbed her arms
and stuck her foot in the water again, this time past the
ankle. Again she looked at the dark windows all around.
Then she peeled off the blouse, tossed it behind her, and
jumped in.

Jean's heart clenched when she hit the water. She kicked
herself back up, gasping for air, and grabbed the ladder.
Tremors twitched across her shoulders. Her toes curled
painfully, then went numb. Jean held to the ladder and
waited for the numbness to spread. She looked up. A plane
was moving slowly across the sky. Jean timed her breathing
to the blinking of its lights, and when she had calmed herself she took a series of deeper and deeper breaths until she
had the one she wanted. Then she pushed off and dove
toward the glowing red triangle at the bottom of the pool.

Her eyes ached. That was all she felt. Jean closed her
fingers around the handlebars and tried to scissor-kick the
bicycle up with her, but when she had it halfway to the
surface it seemed to take on weight, and she had to let it
go. It settled to the bottom without a sound, sending only
a dull shock up through the water. Jean filled her lungs and
went back under. She took hold of the handlebars again.
She dragged the bike along the tiles to the side of the
pool, where she went into a crouch and shoved away hard
from the bottom. Kicking furiously, clawing the water
with her free hand, Jean rose slowly toward the gleaming
chrome of the ladder and just managed to grab the second
rung as the bike began to pull her back down.

She let out the last of her air.

The bike was getting heavy. Jean brought her knees up and got her feet on the lowest rung. She rested a moment. Then she moved her free hand to the rail and began to straighten her legs, pushing herself up toward the light flashing on the surface just above her. She felt her mouth start to open. *No*, she thought, but her mouth opened anyway and Jean was choking when her head broke through to air. She coughed out the water in her throat and then gagged on the chlorine aftertaste until she almost puked. Her eyes burned.

Jean climbed the ladder to where she could work her hips over the edge of the pool and slide forward a bit. She let go of the rail and wiped her face. Her other arm was dead, but she knew the bike was still there because she could feel its weight in her shoulders and back. In a little while she would pull it out. No problem — just as soon as she got herself back together. But until then she couldn't do a thing but lie with her cheek on the cement, and blink her eyes, and savor the cold air that passed through her.

THE MISSING
PERSON

Father Leo started out with the idea of becoming a missionary. He'd read a priest's account of his years among the Aleuts and decided that this was the life for him — trekking from trapper's hut to Indian village, a dog for company, sacramental wine in his knapsack, across snowfields that gleamed like sugar. He knew it would be hard. He would suffer things he could not imagine in that polar solitude. But it was the life he wanted, a life full of risk among people who needed him and were hungry for what he had to give.

Shortly before his ordination he asked to be sent to Alaska. The diocese turned down his request. The local parishes were short of priests and their needs came first. Father Leo was assigned to a parish in West Seattle, where the pastor took an immediate dislike to him and put him on what he called "crone duty" — managing rummage sales, bingo, the Legion of Mary, and visiting sick parishioners in the hospital. Father Leo worked hard at everything he put his hand to. He hoped that the old priest would notice and begin to soften toward him, but that never happened.

He stayed on in the parish. The old priest kept going, though his mind had begun to wander and he could not walk without a stick. He repeated his sermons again and again. There was one story he told at least once a month, about an Irishman who received a visitation from his mother the night after her death, a visit that caused him to change his whole life. He told the story with a brogue, and it went on forever.

The parishioners didn't seem to mind. More of them came every year, and they kept the old priest busy from morning to night. He liked to say that he didn't have time to die. One night he said it at dinner and Father Leo thought, *Make time.* Then he felt so ashamed that he couldn't eat the rest of his meal. But the thought kept coming back.

Finally the old priest did die. Father Leo collected his papers for the diocese and found copies of several reports the old priest had made on him. They were all disparaging, and some of them were untrue. He sat on the floor and read them through carefully. Then he put them down and rubbed his eyes. It was the first warm night of the year. The window was open. A moth fluttered against the screen.

Father Leo was surprised at what he'd found. He couldn't understand why the old priest had hated him. But the more he thought about it, the less strange it seemed. Father Leo had been in love once, before entering the seminary, and remembered the helplessness of it. There had been no reason for him to be in love with the girl; she was no better than other girls he knew, and apart from loving her he didn't like her very much. Still, he probably would have married her if he had not felt even greater helplessness before his conviction that he should become a priest. She was desolate when he told her what he was planning to do, to the point that he nearly changed his mind. Then she lost interest. A few months later she married another man.

Vocation was a mystery, love was a mystery, and Father

Leo supposed that hatred was a mystery. The old priest had been pulled under by it. That was a shame, but Father Leo knew better than to ponder its meaning for him.

A monsignor from the chancery was named to succeed the old priest. Father Leo brooded. He began to fear that he would never get his own parish, and for the first time he considered leaving the priesthood, as most of his friends from the seminary had done. But he never got very far with this thought, because he could not imagine himself as anything other than what he was.

The monsignor asked Father Leo to stay on and teach religion in the parish elementary school. Father Leo agreed. At the end of their interview the monsignor asked if there were any hard feelings.

"Not at all," Father Leo said, and smiled. That night, driving back to the rectory from a visit with his sister, Father Leo began to shake. He was shaking so badly that he pulled onto the shoulder of the road, where he pounded his fist on the dashboard and yelled, "No hard feelings! No hard feelings!"

But he came to like teaching. His students were troubled and cruel to each other but they were still curious about things that mattered: what they should believe in, how they should live. They paid attention to what Father Leo said, and at these moments he felt glad to be where he was.

Every couple of years or so the diocese sent out new books to religion teachers. Father Leo found the changes confusing and stopped trying to keep up. When the books came in he put them on a shelf and forgot about them. That was how he got fired. His classes were inspected by a priest in the education office that sent the books, and afterwards Father Leo received a summons. He went before a committee. After they questioned him, the chairman sent a letter to the monsignor saying that Father Leo's ideas were obsolete and peculiar. The committee suggested that he be replaced.

The monsignor took Father Leo out to dinner at a seafood house and explained the situation to him. The suggestion of the committee was actually a directive, he said. The monsignor had no choice in the matter. But he had been calling around and had found an open position, if Father Leo was interested. Mother Vincent at Star of the Sea needed a new chaplain. Their last chaplain had married one of the nuns. It so happened, the monsignor said, looking into his wine, swirling it gently, that he had done several favors for Mother Vincent in his days at the chancery. In short, if Father Leo wanted the position he could have it. The monsignor lit a cigarette and looked out the window, over the water. Gulls were diving for scraps.

He seemed embarrassed and Father Leo knew why. It was a job for an old priest, or one recovering from something: sickness, alcohol, a breakdown.

"Where will I live?" he asked.

"At the convent," the monsignor said.

Something had gone wrong at Star of the Sea. It was an unhappy place. Some of the sisters were boisterous, and their noise made the silence of the others seem that much deeper. Coming upon these sad, silent nuns in the corridor or on the grounds, Father Leo felt a chill. It was like swimming into a cold pocket in a lake.

Several nuns had left the order. Others were thinking of it. They came to Father Leo and complained about the noise and confusion. They couldn't understand what was happening. Father Leo told them what he told himself: Be patient. But the truth was that his own patience had begun to give out.

He was supposed to be spiritual adviser to the convent. Many of the nuns disregarded him, though. They went their own way. The director of novices described herself as a "Post-Christian" and at Easter sent out cards showing an Indian god ascending to the clouds with arms waving out of his sides like a centipede's. Some held jobs in town. The original idea had been for the nuns to serve the community in some way, but now they did what they wanted to do. One was a disc jockey.

The rowdy nuns ran around together and played pranks. Their jokes were good-natured but often in bad taste, and they didn't know when to stop. A couple of them had stereos and played weird music at night. The hallways echoed with their voices.

They called Father Leo "Padre" or just "Pod." When he walked past them they usually made some crack or asked a cute question. They made racy jokes about Jerry, the fellow Mother Vincent had hired to raise funds. They were always laughing about something.

One evening Father Leo went to Mother Vincent's office and told her, again, that the convent was in trouble. This was his third visit that month and she made it plain that she was not glad to see him. She neither rose to meet him nor invited him to sit down. While he talked she gazed out the open window and rubbed the knuckles of her huge red hands. Father Leo could see that she was listening to the crickets, not to him, and he lost heart.

Mother Vincent was strong, but old and drifting. She had no idea what was going on downstairs. Her office and rooms were on the top floor of the building, separate from the others, and her life took place even farther away than that. She lived in her dream of what the convent was. She believed that it was a perfect song, all voices tuned, sweet and cool and pure, rising and falling in measure. Her strength had hardened around that dream. It was more than Father Leo could contend with.

He broke off, though he hadn't finished what he had come to say. She went on staring out the window at the darkness.

"Father," she said, "I wonder if you are happy with us." He waited.

"Because if you are not happy at Star of the Sea," she went on, "the last thing I would want to do is keep you here." She looked at him. She said, "Is there anywhere else you want to be?"

Father Leo took her meaning, or thought he did. She meant, Is there anywhere else that would have you? He shook his head.

"Of course you hear complaints," she said. "You will always hear complaints. Every convent has its sob-sister element. Myself, I would trade ten wilting pansies for one Sister Gervaise any day. High spirits. A sense of fun. You need a sense of fun in this life, Father."

Mother Vincent drew her chair up to the desk. "If you don't mind my saying so, Father," she said, "you are inclined to take yourself too seriously. You think too much about your own problems. That's because you don't have enough to keep you busy here." She put her hands on the desktop and folded them together. She said that she had a suggestion to make. Jerry, her fund-raiser, needed some help. The convent could not afford to hire another man but she saw no reason why Father Leo couldn't pitch in. It would be good for him. It would be good for everyone.

"I've never done any fund-raising before," Father Leo said. But later that night, back in his room, he began to like the idea. It meant that he would meet new people. He would be doing something different. Most of all, it meant that he would be getting out every day, away from this unhappy place.

Father Leo had coffee with Jerry a few mornings later. Though the weather was warm, Jerry had on a three-piece suit which he kept adjusting. He was nearly as tall as Father Leo but much thicker. There were lines across the front of his vest where the buttons strained. Rings sparkled on his thick, blunt fingers as he moved his hands over the sheets of paper he'd spread on the table. The papers were filled with figures showing what the convent's debts were, and how fast they were growing.

Father Leo hadn't known any of this. It came as a surprise to him that they could owe so much — that it was allowed. He studied the papers. He felt good bending over the table with Jerry, the smell of coffee rising up from the mug in his hand.

"That's not all of it," Jerry said. "Not by a long shot. Let me show you what we're actually looking at here." He took Father Leo on a tour. He pointed out the old pipes, the warped window frames, the cracked foundation. He dug at the crumbling mortar in the walls and even pulled out a brick. He turned a flashlight on pools of scummy water in the vast basement. At the end of the tour Jerry added everything up — debts, operating expenses, and the cost of putting the physical plant back in shape.

Father Leo looked at the figures. He whistled.

"I've seen worse," Jerry said. "Our Lady of Perpetual Help was twice as bad as this, and I had them in the black in two years. It's easy. You go where the money is and you bring the money back."

They were standing beside an empty greenhouse with most of the windows broken out. Shards of glass glittered at their feet. It had rained earlier and now everything seemed unnaturally bright: the grass, the blue of the sky, the white sails of the boats on Puget Sound. The sun was at Father Leo's back, shining into Jerry's face. Jerry squinted as he talked. Father Leo saw that there were little scars under his eyes. His nose was puffy.

"I should tell you," Father Leo said. "I've never raised funds before."

"Nothing to it," Jerry said. "But first you have to make up your mind whether you really want the money. You ask yourself, Is it worth going after or isn't it? Then, if the answer is yes, you go after it." He looked at Father Leo. "So what is it? Yes or no?"

"Yes," Father Leo said.

"All right! That's the big step. The rest is easy. You don't mess around. You don't get hung up on details. You do whatever you have to do and keep going. It's the only way. The question is, can you work like that?" Jerry brushed some brick dust off his jacket. He straightened his vest. He looked down at his shoes, then at Father Leo.

"I think so," Father Leo said.

"You have to be a gunslinger," Jerry said. "No doubts. No pity."

"I understand," Father Leo said.

"All right," Jerry said. "Just so you know how I work. My philosophy." He pulled a flask from his jacket pocket, drank from it, and held it out to Father Leo. "Go on," he said. Father Leo took it. The flask was silver, half-covered with leather, and engraved with initials below the neck. They weren't Jerry's initials. The liquor burned. Father Leo became aware of the sun on the back of his neck, the sighing of the trees. They each had another drink, then Jerry put the flask away. "Cognac," he said. "Napoleon's brand. So, what do you think? Partners?"

"Partners," Father Leo said.

"Bueno," Jerry said. He slapped his leg and brought his hand up like a pistol. "Okay," he said. "Let's ride."

The plan was for Father Leo to go with Jerry and watch how he approached potential donors. Then, once he got the hang of it, he could go out on his own. Jerry coached him on the way to their first interview. He said that the big thing was to make it personal. Nobody wanted to hear about old furnaces. You had to do your homework, you had to know your man — in this case, your woman. Here they had a lady who went to Lourdes every year. She'd been to Lourdes more than twenty times. That meant she had a special interest in crippled people. She had a big heart and she had money. Going to France wasn't like going to Mexico.

The woman was standing at the door when they arrived. Father Leo followed Jerry up the walk, moving slowly, because Jerry had assumed what appeared to be a painful limp. He had endless trouble with the steps but refused the woman's help. "I can manage," he said. "There's plenty worse off than me. I just think of them and it's easy."

Jerry did all the talking when they got inside. Now and then the woman looked over at Father Leo, but he would not meet her eyes. Jerry was describing a number of projects that Star of the Sea had developed for the handicapped, all of them imaginary. He implied that most of the nuns were devoted to this particular work and that he himself had been rescued by their efforts. Jerry's voice cracked. He looked away for a moment, then went on. When he finished, the woman served tea and wrote out a check.

Not everyone they visited gave them money. One old man laughed in their faces when Jerry told him that the convent had been built on orders from the Blessed Mother, and that she was taking a personal interest in the fund drive. When the old man stopped laughing he threw them out. "You must take me for an idiot," he said.

Not everyone gave, but most people did. Jerry would say anything. He said that the convent helped orphans, lepers, Navahos, earthquake victims, even pandas and seals. There was no end to what he would do.

Jerry had a saying: "If you want the apples, you have to shake the tree."

Father Leo knew that he should disapprove of Jerry's methods, but he didn't. That is, he felt no disapproval. The people they visited lived in Broadmoor and Windermere. They had plenty of money, too much money. It was good for them to share it. Anyway, Jerry was a performer, not a liar. Lying was selfish, furtive, low. What Jerry did was reckless and grand, for a good cause.

Father Leo did not want to go out on his own. He would never be able to carry on the way Jerry did in front of complete strangers. He did not have the courage. He would fail.

Besides, he was having the time of his life. Jerry called him "Slim," and he liked that. He liked getting into Jerry's big car and driving through the convent gate with no idea what would happen that day. He looked forward to the lunches they ate downtown — club sandwiches, fruit platters, big salads covered with diced cheese and ham. Then the coffee afterwards, and one of Jerry's stories about his days in the navy. Father Leo came to need these pleasures, most of all the pleasure of watching Jerry have it his way with people who were used to having it their way.

As it happened they did not split up after all. Jerry tallied their take for the month and decided that they should stick together. The receipts were almost double the average. He said that as a team they were unbeatable. He had the blarney and Father Leo had the collar, which Jerry called "The Persuader."

They would go on as before. Father Leo's job was just to sit there. He didn't have to say anything. If someone should look at him in a questioning way, all he had to do was close his eyes. No nodding. No murmuring.

"We'll rake it in," Jerry said, and they did.

When they finished their rounds, Jerry and Father Leo usually had a drink at a fern bar on the wharf. They sat in a booth and Jerry told stories about his life. He'd sold cars and worked as a private detective. For two years he had been a professional fighter. He had been everywhere and seen everything. In Singapore he had witnessed a murder, one man shooting another man right in the face. "Just like you'd shoot a can," Jerry said. Later he'd heard the men were brothers. He had seen men make love to each other on board ship. In Dakar he'd watched a woman with knobs where her arms should have been paint pictures of sailors, take their money, and give change all with the toes of her feet. He had seen children chained to a wall, for sale.

So he said. Father Leo did not believe all the stories Jerry told him. Roughly speaking, he believed about half of what he heard. That was fine with him. He didn't mind having his leg pulled. He thought it was the sort of thing men did in lumber camps and on ships — sitting around, swapping lies.

Just before Thanksgiving they had a meeting with a vice president of Boeing. The man wore sunglasses during the interview. It was hard to tell what he was thinking. Father Leo guessed that he was trying to keep his temper, because in his opinion Jerry had chosen the wrong line to follow. Jerry was going on about missiles and bombers and instruments of destruction. He suggested that the man had a lot to make amends for. Father Leo wanted to get out. When Jerry was through, the vice president sat there behind his desk and stared at them. He said nothing. Father Leo became uncomfortable, then angry. This was obviously some technique the vice president used to bully his subordinates. "You ought to be ashamed of yourself," he said.

The vice president suddenly bent over. He buried his face in the crook of his arm. "You don't know the half of it," he said. His shoulders began to jerk.

Jerry looked at Father Leo and gave the thumbs-up. He went around the desk and stood behind the man. "There, there," he said.

The vice president stopped crying. He took off his sunglasses and wiped his eyes. "I needed that," he said. "By God, I needed that." He went into the adjoining room and came back with a plastic garbage bag. It was full of money, but he would not let Jerry count it in the office or give him a receipt. He insisted that the gift remain anonymous. As he showed them out of the office, he took Father Leo by the sleeve. "Pray for me," he said.

They counted the money in the car. It came to seven thousand dollars, all in twenties. Jerry locked it in the trunk and they went to the fern bar to celebrate. Jerry's cheeks were red and they grew redder as he drank cognac after cognac. Father Leo did not try to keep up with him, but he drank more than usual and became a little giddy. Now and then the young people at the bar turned and smiled at him. He could see that they were thinking, *What a jolly priest!* That was all right. He wanted to look like someone with good news, not like someone with bad news.

Jerry held up his glass. "The team," he said, and Father Leo said, "The team." They toasted each other. "I'll tell you what," Jerry said. "We have a bonus coming, and I'm going to see that we get it if I have to break Vincent's arm." When Father Leo asked what kind of a bonus Jerry had in mind, Jerry said, "How about Thanksgiving in Vegas?"

"Las Vegas?"

"You bet. We're riding a streak. We've made plenty for Vincent, why shouldn't we make a little for ourselves?"

Father Leo knew that Mother Vincent would never agree, so he said, "Sure. Why not?" and they touched glasses again.

"Slim, you're something," Jerry said. "You're really something." He shook his head. "You're as bad as I am."

Father Leo smiled.

Jerry said, "I'm going to tell you something I've never told anyone before. Maybe I shouldn't even tell you." He lit a cigar and blew smoke at the ceiling. "Hell with it," he said. He leaned forward. In a low voice he told Father Leo that Jerry was not his real name. Royce, his last name, was also made up. He'd taken it from Rolls-Royce, his favorite car.

It happened like this. He had been selling insurance in San Diego a few years back and some of his clients complained because they didn't get the benefits he had promised them. It was his own fault. He had overdone it, laid it on too thick. He would be the first to admit that. Anyway, he'd had to change names. There was no choice, not if he wanted to keep working and stay out of jail. The worst of it was that his wife left town with their son. He hadn't seen them since, had no idea where they were. That hurt. But in some ways, looking back on it, he thought that it was for the best. They didn't get along and she was holding him back. Always criticizing. If she'd had her way he'd still be in the navy, pulling down a hundred and forty dollars a month. "She loved it," he said. "So did I, at least for a while. We were just kids. We didn't know from Adam."

Jerry looked at the people in the next booth, then at Father Leo. He said, "Do you want to know what my real name is?"

Father Leo nodded. But just when Jerry was about to speak he interrupted. "Maybe you'd better not tell me," he said. "It's probably not such a good idea."

Jerry looked disappointed. Father Leo felt bad, but he didn't want that kind of power, the power to send a man to jail. He was also afraid that Jerry would start wondering about him all the time, whether he could be trusted, whether he would tell. It would spoil everything. They sat for a while without talking. Father Leo knew that it was his turn. He should open up and talk about himself for a change. But there was nothing to tell. He had no stories. Not one.

Outside the window it was raining. Cars went past with a hissing sound. Father Leo said, "Jerry?" His throat felt scratchy. He did not know what he would say next.

Jerry moved in his seat and looked at him.

"You've got to keep this to yourself," Father Leo said.

Jerry pulled his thumb and forefinger across his lips as if he were closing a zipper. "It stops here," he said.

"All right," Father Leo said. He took a sip from his drink. Then he started talking. He said that when he was a senior in high school he had been waiting for a bus when he heard someone scream across the road. He ran over and saw a woman on her knees, hanging on to the belt of a man with a purse in his hand. The man turned and kicked the woman in the face. "I guess I went berserk," Father Leo said. The next thing he knew, the police were dragging him off the man's body. The man was dead. Father Leo said that they'd had to pry his fingers off the man's throat, one by one.

"Jesus," Jerry said. "Is that the reason you became a priest?"

Father Leo looked out the window. "One of the reasons," he said.

"Jesus," Jerry said again. He looked young and amazed, wide-eyed as he must have been years ago, before his name was Jerry. His eyes were watery; when he tried to smile, his mouth wouldn't hold the shape. He reached out and squeezed Father Leo's shoulder. He squeezed it again, then got up and went to the bar.

Oh, no, Father Leo thought. What have I done?

Jerry came back with fresh drinks. He sat down and slid one over to Father Leo. His eyes were still misty. "Vegas," he said, and raised his glass.

"Vegas," Father Leo said.

Mother Vincent gave them the bonus. Thanksgiving weekend in Las Vegas, all expenses paid — air fare, hotel, meals, and a hundred dollars apiece in gambling coupons. The trip was arranged at discount by a nun who worked as a travel agent.

"Something is going to happen," Jerry told Father Leo as their plane banked over the desert. "I feel it. Something big. We're going to come home with gold in our saddle-bags. Hey, don't laugh," he said. "Don't ever laugh about that."

"I can't help it," Father Leo said.

"Be serious, Slim. We are two serious hombres on a roll and we are about to bust this town wide open. We'll never work again. It is written." He leaned past Father Leo and looked down at the cluster of lights that turned below them in the darkness.

There was a commotion in the hotel lobby when they

arrived. A woman was yelling that her room had been broken into. Two men in fringed leather jackets tried to soothe her and finally managed to lead her to an office behind the registration desk, where she began to yell again. Father Leo could hear every word from where he stood in line. He picked up the room keys and meal coupons and gambling chips, and turned around just in time to see Jerry win twelve dollars at one of the quarter slots by the Hertz counter. The coins slid out of the machine onto the tile floor with a steady ringing sound and rolled in every direction. Jerry got down on his hands and knees and crawled after them. Nobody paid any attention except a red-haired man in silver pants who went over to Jerry and touched his shoulder, then hurried away.

They ate dinner at the hotel, the only place where their coupons were good. Jerry spent his winnings on a bottle of wine, to celebrate. He couldn't get over it — a jackpot the first time around. "Figure the odds on that," he said. "It's an omen. It means we can't lose."

"I'm not much of a gambler," Father Leo said. It was true. He had never won a bet in his life. The chips they'd been given were negotiable and he intended to cash them in just before he left and buy his sister something nice for Christmas, something he would not usually be able to afford. For now they were squirreled away in the bottom of his suitcase.

"Who's talking about gambling?" Jerry said. "I'm talking about fate. You know what I mean."

"I guess I don't," Father Leo said. "Not really."

"Sure you do. What about the guy you killed? It was fate that put you there. It was fate that you became a priest."

Father Leo saw how the lie had grown. It had taken on a meaning and the meaning was false. He felt tired of himself. He said, "Jerry, it isn't true."

"What isn't true?"

"I never killed anyone."

Jerry smiled at him. "Come off it."

"I've never even been in a fight," Father Leo said.

Jerry leaned forward. "Look," he said, "you shouldn't feel guilty about it. It was that kind of a situation. I would have done the same thing in your shoes. That's what I told Sister Gervaise."

"No," Father Leo said. "You didn't."

"Don't worry," Jerry said. "She promised not to tell anyone. The thing is, she made a smart remark about you and I wanted to set her straight. It worked, too. She went white as a ghost. She looked about ready to hemorrhage. You should have seen her."

"She's a gossip," Father Leo said. "She'll tell everyone. She'll tell Mother Vincent."

"I made her promise," Jerry said. "She gave her word."

"So did you."

Jerry put a coupon on the table. He ground out his cigar. "This conversation isn't going anywhere," he said. "What's done is done. We're in Get Rich City now, and it's time to start raking it in."

There was a small casino on the other side of the lobby. Jerry suggested that they start there. He sat down at the blackjack table. Father Leo moved up and watched the play. He was pretending to study Jerry's tactics, but none of it made any sense to him. He could only think of Sister Gervaise turning white. He felt as if he must be turning white himself. "I'm going upstairs," he told Jerry. "I'll be back in a little while."

Father Leo sat on the balcony outside his room. In the courtyard below there was a turquoise pool lit by underwater lights. He gripped the armrests of his chair. He could not stop thinking of Sister Gervaise, stricken and pale. What was he supposed to do? He couldn't have Mother Vincent and the others believing that he had killed a man. It would terrify them. On the other hand, he didn't want them to think that he went around telling crazy lies about himself. In its own way, that was just as bad. He put his head in his hands. He couldn't think. Finally he gave up and went back downstairs.

Another man had taken Jerry's place at the blackjack table. Father Leo couldn't find Jerry at any of the other tables and he wasn't at the bar or in the lobby. On the chance that he'd gone to his room, Father Leo called upstairs on the house phone. There was no answer. He went outside and stood under the awning beside the doorman.

A greyhound wearing a sweater and pulling an old woman behind him stopped and lifted his leg over a small border of flowers in front of the hotel. While the dog peed, the woman glared at the doorman. He clasped his white-gloved hands behind his back and looked up at the sky.

Along the street colored lights flashed names and pictures. Farther down was a sign that must have been twenty feet high, showing a line of chorus girls in cowboy boots and bikinis. Every so often they kicked their legs this way and that. They were smiling, and each tooth was a little light. People spilled over into the street, moving in different directions. They shouted back and forth and ignored the cars that honked at them.

"Thanksgiving," the doorman said. Then he said something that Father Leo couldn't hear because of the noise.

There was no point in looking for Jerry in that crowd. Father Leo went back inside and took a seat at the bar. From the bar he could keep an eye on both the lobby and the casino. He sipped at his drink and glanced around. A muscular-looking girl with tattooed snakes coiling up her bare arms was poking out numbers on a punchboard. Two pudgy Indian men wearing identical Hawaiian shirts sat silently side by side. At the end of the bar a small, red-haired woman was emptying her purse and spreading its contents in front of her. She dipped her hand into her purse with the predatory crispness of a robin driving its beak into the ground, and Father Leo found himself watching her to see what she came up with. At last she found what she was after — cigarettes — and lit one. She pursed her lips and blew out a long stream of smoke. Then she noticed that Father Leo was looking at her. She looked back at him. Father Leo gave a little nod, and lowered his eyes. Soon afterwards he finished his drink and left the bar.

Father Leo sat in the lobby for an hour, reading newspapers. Every time someone came in he looked up. When he felt himself getting sleepy he went to the desk and talked to the clerk. Jerry had left his key, but no message. "That's strange," Father Leo said. He walked across the lobby to the elevator. The red-haired woman from the bar was standing inside, holding the door for him. "What floor?" she asked.

"Five. Thank you."

"Coincidence," she said. "That's my floor too." She and Father Leo stared at each other's reflections in the mirrored wall. She was about his age, older than he'd thought. There were wrinkles around her mouth. He saw that she was badly sunburned except for a white circle around each eye. He could almost feel the heat coming off her pink skin. She was tapping one foot.

"Been here long?" she asked.

He shook his head. The elevator stopped and they got out. She walked beside him down the corridor. "I flew in two days ago," she said. "I don't mind telling you I've been having a ball." When Father Leo put his key into the lock she read the number on his door. "Five-fifteen. That's easy to remember. I always leave work at five-fifteen. I could leave at five but I like it when everyone's gone. I like to just sit and look out the window. It's so peaceful."

"Good night," Father Leo said. She was still talking when he closed the door. He sat for a time on his balcony. There were high palms around the pool, and overhead a bright crescent moon. Father Leo thought of a band of marauders camped by a well in the desert, roasting a lamb over a spitting fire, the silver moon reflected in the chasing of their long inlaid rifles. Veiled women moving here and there in silence, doing as they were told.

Before he went to bed Father Leo called the desk. Jerry's key was still on its hook.

"It's only twelve-thirty," the clerk said. "You could try later."

Father Leo turned out the lights. The ceiling sparkled. He was staring at it when he thought he heard a sound at the door. He sat up. "Who's there?" he called. When no one answered he said, "Jerry?" The sound did not come again.

On his way to breakfast the next morning Father Leo stopped by the front desk. Jerry still hadn't come in. Father Leo left a message — "I'm in the coffee shop" — and when he finished eating he changed it to "Went out. Be back soon."

Though it was just after eleven, the street was already jammed with people. A dry breeze blew, bearing a faint smell that made Father Leo think of the word *sage*. Off in the distance purple mountains floated on a shimmering lake of blue. The sidewalk glowed.

For the rest of the morning Father Leo searched the casinos. He thought that Jerry might have wandered in and got caught up in one of those games that went on forever. But he didn't see him, or if he saw him he didn't recognize him. That was possible. There were so many people. Bent over their machines, faces fixed and drained by the hot lights, they all began to look the same to Father Leo. He couldn't tell who he was looking at and it wore him out to try. At two o'clock he went back to the hotel, intending to search the casinos again after he'd eaten lunch.

He sat at the counter and watched the crowd move past outside. It was noisy in the coffee shop, which was full of Japanese men in business suits. They all wore cowboy hats and string ties with roadrunner clasps. At the back of the room a bunch of them were playing slot machines. There weren't enough machines to go around so they took turns, standing behind each other in little lines. One of them hit a jackpot and all the others, including those at the tables, stopped talking and applauded.

"If it isn't five-fifteen." The red-haired woman from the night before sat down at the next stool and offered Father Leo a package of Salems with one cigarette sticking halfway out. He shook his head. She slid the cigarette from the pack, tapped it once on the countertop, and put it in the ashtray. "For later," she said. "I can't smoke on an empty stomach." Her face had turned the color of brick. It was painful for Father Leo to look at her and to think of how hot and tight her skin must feel, and how it must hurt her to keep smiling the way she did.

"By the way," she said, "I'm Sandra."

Father Leo did not want to know this woman's name and he did not want her to know his name. But she kept waiting. "Slim," he said.

"Then you must be a Westerner."

He nodded. "Seattle and thereabouts."

She said, "I met a fellow in the casino named Will. In Chicago you just don't hear names like that. Will and Slim. It's so different. I'm talking too much, aren't I?"

"Not at all," Father Leo said.

The waitress took Sandra's order and slipped Father Leo's check under his plate. He picked it up and looked at it.

"Let me treat you to a refill," Sandra said, pointing at his coffee cup.

He stood. "No thanks," he said. "I've got to be going. Much obliged."

Jerry hadn't called in yet or used his key. Father Leo left another message for him and went upstairs to his room. He thought he would lie down for a while before making another tour of the casinos. When he stepped inside he saw that his suitcase was open, though he could remember closing it. On the table next to the suitcase a cigarette was coming apart in a glass of water.

He knelt and went through the suitcase. He sat back for a moment, caught his breath, and searched the suitcase again. The chips were gone. Father Leo flushed the cigarette down the toilet and dropped the glass in the wastebasket. He could feel the blood pulse in his temples, its beat strong and uneven, surprising him and shaking him as if he were hollow. He sat on the bed. The hollowness spread downwards into his chest and legs. When he stood he rose up and up. He saw his shoes side by side on the rug, a long way below. He walked over to the balcony door and back. Then he began to talk to himself.

The things Father Leo said didn't make any sense. They were only noises. He kept pacing the room. He struck himself over the heart. He gripped his shirt in both hands and tore it open to his waist. He struck himself again. Back and forth he walked.

The sounds he made grew soft and distant, then stopped. Father Leo stood there. He looked down at the front of his shirt. One button was missing. Another hung by a thread. The room was hot and still smelled of the thief's cigarette. Father Leo slid open the glass door and went out onto the balcony. The desert was hidden by casinos but he could feel it all around him and taste its dryness in the breeze. The breeze ruffled the surface of the pool below, breaking the sun's reflection. The broken light glittered on the water.

When the desk clerk saw Father Leo coming, he shook his head. Father Leo walked up to him anyway. "No message?"

"Not a thing," the desk clerk said. He went back to his magazine.

Father Leo had meant to report the theft, but now he didn't see the point. The police would come and make him fill out a lot of forms. They would ask him questions; he felt uneasy about that, about explaining his presence in Las Vegas.

For the rest of the afternoon he went up and down the street, looking for Jerry. Once he thought he saw him going into a casino but it turned out to be somebody else. Father Leo returned to the hotel. He didn't feel like going back to his room, so he bought a copy of *Time* and went out to the pool.

Two young girls were doing cannonballs off the diving board. Father Leo tried to read an article about the creation of the universe but he couldn't keep his mind on it. After a time he gave up and watched the girls, who sensed his attention. They began to show off. First they did swan dives. Then one of them tried a flip. She hit the water with a loud crack, flat on her stomach. Father Leo started out of his chair, but she seemed to be all right. She pulled herself up the ladder and left the courtyard, crying. Her friend walked carefully out to the end of the board, turned around, bounced twice, and executed a perfect backward flip. Then she walked away from the pool, feet slapping on the wet cement.

"Coincidence," Sandra said. "Looks like we've got the pool to ourselves." She was standing beside the next chair, looking down at him. She stepped out of her high-heeled clogs and took off her robe.

"You shouldn't be out here," Father Leo said. "Not with that burn of yours."

"This is my last day," she said. "I wanted to catch the sunset."

Father Leo looked up. The sun was just touching the roof of the hotel across from them. It looked like another sign.

Sandra sat down and took a bottle of baby oil out of her tote bag. She rubbed the oil along her arms and across her chest, under the halter of her bathing suit. Then she raised her legs one at a time and slowly oiled them until they glistened. They were deep red. "So," she said, "where's your wife?"

"I'm not married."

"Me either," she said.

Father Leo closed his magazine and sat up.

"What shows have you been to?" she asked.

"None."

"You should go," she said. "The dancers are so beautiful. I don't think I've ever seen such beautiful men and women in my whole life. Do you like to dance?"

Father Leo shook his head.

Sandra drew her legs up. She rested her chin between her knees. "What do you like?"

Father Leo was about to say "I like peace and quiet," but he stopped himself. She was lonely. There was no reason to hurt her feelings. "I like to read," he said. "Music. Good music, not weird music. Eating in restaurants. Talking to friends."

"Me too," Sandra said. "Those are the same things I like." She lowered the back of the deck chair and rolled onto her stomach. She rubbed baby oil over her shoulders, then held the bottle out toward Father Leo. "Could you give me a hand?" she said.

He saw that she wanted him to oil her back, which looked swollen and painful, glowing in the little sun that was left. "I'm afraid I can't do that," he said.

"Oh," she said. She put the bottle down. "Sorry I asked."

"I'm a priest," he said.

"That's a new one," she said, not looking at him. "A priest named Slim."

"Slim is my nickname," he said.

"Sure," she said. "Your nickname. What kind of priest are you, anyway?"

Father Leo began to explain but she cut him off. "You're no priest," she said. She sat up and began stuffing things into her tote bag — lighter, cigarettes, baby oil, sunglasses. She put her robe on and stepped into her clogs. "If you were a priest, you wouldn't have let me go on like I did. You wouldn't have let me make a fool of myself." She stood there, looking down at him. "What are you, anyway?"

"I came here with a friend," Father Leo said. "He's been gone ever since last night. I don't have any idea where he is. This isn't a very good explanation," Father Leo added. "I'm a little confused right now."

"I don't know what you are," she said, "but if you come near me again I'll scream."

Father Leo thought of calling the police, but he was afraid that if they did find Jerry they would discover his real name and put him in prison. He looked up the numbers of all the hospitals in town. There were seven. None of them had a Jerry Royce registered, but at Desert Springs the nurse who took the call said that on the previous night they had admitted a John Doe with what she called a "sucking chest wound." Father Leo asked for a description of the man, but she did not have his file and the line to Intensive Care was busy. "It's always busy," she told him. If you're in town, the simplest thing is to just come over."

But when Father Leo arrived at Intensive Care, he discovered that the John Doe was dead. He had died that afternoon and they had sent his body to the morgue. Father Leo put his hands on the desk. "The morgue?" he said.

The nurse nodded. "We have a picture. Would you like to see it?"

"I guess I'd better," Father Leo said. He was afraid to look at the picture but he didn't feel ready for a trip to the morgue. The nurse opened a folder and took out a large glossy photograph and handed it to him. The face was that of a boy with narrow features. His eyes were open, staring without defiance or shyness into the blaze of the flash. Father Leo knew that the boy had died before the picture was taken. He gave the picture back.

The nurse looked at it. "Not your friend?" she asked.

He shook his head. "What happened?"

"He was stabbed." She put the folder away.

"Did they catch the person who did it?"

"Probably not," she said. "We get over a hundred murders a year in town."

On his way back to the hotel Father Leo watched the crowd through the window of the cab. A group of sailors ran across the street. The one in front was throwing coins over his shoulder and the rest were jumping for them. Signs flashed. People's faces pulsed with reflected light.

Father Leo bent forward. "I just heard that you get over a hundred murders a year in town. Is that true?"

"I suppose it's possible," the cabby said. "This place has its drawbacks, all right. But Utica's a damn sight worse.

They've got almost two feet of snow right now and there's more on the way."

At half-past two in the morning Jerry called. He was sorry about the mix-up, but he could explain everything. It turned out that while Father Leo was upstairs that first night Jerry had met a fellow on his way to a poker game outside town. It was a private game. The players were rich and there was no limit. They'd had to leave right away, so Jerry wasn't able to tell Father Leo. And after he got there he'd had no chance to call. The game was that intense. Incredible amounts of money had changed hands. It was still going on; he'd just broken off to catch a few winks and let Father Leo know that he wouldn't be going back to Seattle the next morning. He couldn't, not now. Jerry had lost every penny of his own savings, the seven thousand dollars from the man at Boeing, and some other cash he had held back. "I feel bad," he said. "I know this is going to put you in an awkward position."

"I think you ought to come home," Father Leo said. "We can work this thing out."

"They'll throw the book at me," Jerry said.

"No, they won't. I won't let them."

"Get serious. Vincent'll have me for dinner."

"She doesn't have to know it was you," Father Leo said. "I'll tell her I took it."

Jerry didn't answer right away. Finally he said, "She'd never believe you."

"Why not? She already thinks I'm a killer."

Jerry laughed. "Slim, you're something. Thanks, but no thanks. I still have four hundred left. I've been down further than that and bounced back. I'm just getting warmed up."

"Jerry, listen."

"Haven't you ever had the feeling that you're bound to win?" Jerry asked. "Like you've been picked out and you'll get taken care of no matter what?"

"Sure," Father Leo said, "I've had that feeling. It doesn't mean a damn thing."

"That's what you say. I happen to feel differently about it."

"For God's sake, Jerry, use your head. Come home."

But it was no good. Jerry said good-bye and hung up. Father Leo sat on the edge of the bed. The telephone rang again. He picked it up and said, "Jerry?"

It wasn't Jerry, though. It was Sandra. "I'm sorry if I woke you up," she said.

"Sandra," he said. "What on earth do you want?"

"Are you really a priest?" she asked.

"What kind of a question is that? What do you mean by calling me at this hour?" Father Leo knew that he had every right to be angry, but he wasn't, not really. The sound of his own voice, fussy and peevish, embarrassed him. "Yes," he said.

"Oh, thank God. I'm so frightened."

He waited.

"Someone's been trying to get into my room," she said. "At least I think they have. I could have been dreaming," she added.

"You should call the police."

"I already thought of that," she said. "What would they do? They'd come in and stand around and then they'd go away. And there I'd be."

"I don't know how I could help," Father Leo said.

"You could stay."

"My friend still isn't back," Father Leo said. "We have to leave tomorrow morning and I should be here in case he calls. What if you were dreaming?"

"Please," she said.

Father Leo slammed his fist into the pillow. "Of course," he said. "Of course, I'll be right there."

After Sandra unlocked the door she told Father Leo to wait a second. Then she called, "Okay. Come on in." She was wearing a blue nightgown. She slid into bed and pulled the covers up to her waist. "Please don't look at me," she said. "And in case you wondered, I'm not making this up. I'm not that desperate for company. Almost but not quite."

There were two beds in the room, with a night table in between. Father Leo sat at the foot of the other bed. He looked at her. Her face was red and puffy. She had white stuff on her nose.

"I'm a sight," she said.

"You should have that burn looked at when you get home."

She shrugged. "It's going to peel whatever I do. In a couple of weeks I'll be back to normal." She tried to smile and gave it up. "I thought I'd at least come home with a tan. This has been the worst vacation. It's been one thing after another." She picked at the covers. "My second night here I lost over three hundred dollars. Do you know how long it takes me to save three hundred dollars?"

"This is an awful place," Father Leo said. "I don't know why anybody comes here."

"That's no mystery," Sandra said. "When you reach a certain point it's the logical place to come."

"The whole thing is fixed," Father Leo said.

Sandra shrugged. "At a certain point that doesn't matter."

Father Leo went over to the sliding glass door. He opened it and stepped out onto the balcony. The night was cold. A mist hung over the glowing blue surface of the pool.

"You'll catch your death out there," Sandra called.

Father Leo went back inside and closed the door. He was restless. The room smelled of coconut oil.

"I have a confession to make," Sandra said. "It wasn't a coincidence when I came out to the pool today. I saw you down there."

Father Leo sat in the chair next to the TV. He rubbed his eyes. "Did somebody really try to break into the room?"

"I thought so," Sandra said. "Can't you tell I'm scared?"

"Yes," he said.

"Then what difference does it make?"

"None," Father Leo said.

"This has been the worst vacation," Sandra said. "I won't tell you all the things that happened to me. Let's just say the only good thing that's happened to me is meeting you."

"This is a terrible place," Father Leo said. "It's dangerous, and everything is set up so you can't win."

"Some people win," she said.

"That's the theory. I haven't seen any winners. Do you mind if I use your phone?"

Sandra smoked and watched Father Leo while he talked to the desk clerk. Jerry had not called back. Father Leo left Sandra's room number and hung up.

"You told him you were here?" she said. "I wonder what he'll think."

"He can think whatever he wants to think."

"He probably isn't thinking anything," Sandra said. "I'll bet he's seen it all."

Father Leo nodded. "I wouldn't be surprised."

"It's strange," she said. "Usually, when I'm about to go home from a vacation, I get excited — even if I've had a great time. This year I just feel sad. How about you? Are you looking forward to going home?"

"Not much," Father Leo said.

"Why not? What's it like where you live?"

Father Leo thought of the noise in the refectory, Sister Gervaise shrieking at one of her own wisecracks. Then he saw her face go white as she listened to the lie he'd told Jerry. It would be all over the convent by now, and there was no way to undo it. When you heard a story like that it became the truth about the person it was spoken of. Denials would only make it seem more true.

He would have to live with it. And that meant that everything was going to change. He saw how it would be. The hallways empty at night and quiet. The sisters falling silent as he walked past them, their eyes downcast.

"What are you smiling at?" Sandra asked.

He shook his head. "Nothing. Just a thought."

"To get back to what we were talking about," Sandra said. "Some people do win. You just have to be lucky. A friend of mine met her husband at the dentist's, of all places. If either he or my friend hadn't made an appointment for that particular morning, they wouldn't have met. If the dentist hadn't taken so long with the patient he was working on they wouldn't have started talking and discovered all the things they have in common. But they did. It can happen."

Sandra stubbed her cigarette out. "The way I've been

acting, you must think I'm completely pathetic. I just want you to know that I'm not."

"I never thought that," Father Leo said.

"Yeah, yeah. You'll say anything to keep me quiet."

Father Leo made sounds of denial.

"I'm not a pathetic person," Sandra said. "I have a life. It's just that with one thing and another I was feeling low, and you struck a chord."

"You don't know me, Sandra."

"Not in the usual way, maybe. But I recognize you, the kind of person you are. Intelligent. Kind. Gallant."

"Gallant," Father Leo said.

Sandra nodded. "You're here, aren't you?"

A group of people went past the door, talking loudly. When it was quiet again, Sandra said, "Is it okay if I ask you a personal question?"

"I guess so," Father Leo said. "Sure. Why not?"

"Do you think you could love me? If the circumstances were changed?"

"The circumstances aren't going to change," Father Leo said.

"I understand that. I understand that absolutely. But speaking in a hypothetical way, do you think you could? Don't worry about hurting my feelings — I'm just curious."

Hypothetically, Father Leo supposed it was possible for him to love anyone. But she didn't really mean that. He thought about it. "Yes," he said.

"What for? What is it about me that you would love if you loved me?" She clasped her arms around her knees, and watched him.

"It's hard to put into words," Father Leo said.

Sandra said, "You don't have to." She shook another cigarette out of the pack, stared at it, and put it down on the night table.

"I like the way you talk," Father Leo said. "Straight out — just what's on your mind."

She nodded. "I do that, all right. Let the chips fall where they may."

"Your spirit," Father Leo said. "Coming here all alone the way you did."

"I got a good deal on the trip."

"So did I," Father Leo said.

They both laughed.

"I thought of going home early," Sandra said, "but once I start something I have to finish it. I have to take it to the end and see how it turns out, even if it turns out awful."

"I know what you mean," Father Leo said. "I'm the same way."

Sandra yawned. "So what else do you like about me?"

"How friendly you are. The way you listen."

She leaned back against the pillow.

"Your eyes."

"My eyes? Really?"

"You have beautiful eyes."

Father Leo went on. He did not think, he just listened to himself. His voice made a cool sound in the stuffy room. After a time Sandra whispered, "You won't leave, will you?"

"I'll be right here," he said.

She slept. Father Leo turned off the lights and moved his chair in front of the door. If anyone tried to break in, he would be in the way. They would have to get past him.

He sat and listened. Every so often, faintly, he heard the

elevator open at the end of the hall. Then he tried to hear
the voices of people who got out, to see if they were men or
women. Whenever he heard a man's voice, or no voice at
all, he tensed. He listened for sounds in the corridor.
Several people went by Sandra's door. Nobody stopped.

The only sounds in the room were his own and Sandra's
breathing; hers ragged, his deep, almost silent.

After a few hours of this he began to drift. Finally he
caught himself dozing off, and went outside onto the
balcony. A few stars still glimmered. The breeze stirred
the fronds of the palm trees. The palms were black against
the purple sky. The moon was white.

Father Leo stood against the railing, chilled awake by
the breeze. A car horn honked, a small sound in the silence.
He listened for it to come again but it didn't, and the
silence seemed to grow. Again he felt the desert all around
him. He thought of a coyote loping home with a rabbit
dangling from its mouth, yellow eyes aglow.

Father Leo rubbed his arms. The cold began to get to
him and he went back inside.

The walls turned from blue to grey. A telephone started
ringing in the room above. There were heavy steps.

Sandra turned. She said something in her sleep. Then
she turned again.

"It's all right," Father Leo said. "I'm here."

SAY YES

They were doing the dishes, his wife washing while he dried. He'd washed the night before. Unlike most men he knew, he really pitched in on the housework. A few months earlier he'd overheard a friend of his wife's congratulate her on having such a considerate husband, and he thought, *I try*. Helping out with the dishes was a way he had of showing how considerate he was.

They talked about different things and somehow got on the subject of whether white people should marry black people. He said that all things considered, he thought it was a bad idea.

"Why?" she asked.

Sometimes his wife got this look where she pinched her brows together and bit her lower lip and stared down at something. When he saw her like this he knew he should keep his mouth shut, but he never did. Actually it made him talk more. She had that look now.

"Why?" she asked again, and stood there with her hand inside a bowl, not washing it but just holding it above the water.

"Listen," he said, "I went to school with blacks and I've worked with blacks and lived on the same street with blacks and we've always gotten along just fine. I don't need you coming along now and implying that I'm a racist."

"I didn't imply anything," she said, and began washing

the bowl again, turning it around in her hand as though she were shaping it. "I just don't see what's wrong with a white person marrying a black person, that's all."

"They don't come from the same culture as we do. Listen to them sometime — they even have their own language. That's okay with me, I *like* hearing them talk" — he did; for some reason it always made him feel happy — "but it's different. A person from their culture and a person from our culture could never really *know* each other."

"Like you know me?" his wife asked.

"Yes. Like I know you."

"But if they love each other," she said. She was washing faster now, not looking at him.

Oh boy, he thought. He said, "Don't take my word for it. Look at the statistics. Most of those marriages break up."

"Statistics." She was piling dishes on the drainboard at a terrific rate, just swiping at them with the cloth. Many of them were greasy, and there were flecks of food between the tines of the forks. "All right," she said, "what about foreigners? I suppose you think the same thing about two foreigners getting married."

"Yes," he said, "as a matter of fact I do. How can you understand someone who comes from a completely different background?"

"Different," said his wife. "Not the same, like us."

"Yes, different," he snapped, angry with her for resorting to this trick of repeating his words so that they sounded crass, or hypocritical. "These are dirty," he said, and dumped all the silverware back into the sink.

The water had gone flat and grey. She stared down at it, her lips pressed tight together, then plunged her hands under the surface. "Oh!" she cried, and jumped back. She took her right hand by the wrist and held it up. Her thumb was bleeding.

"Ann, don't move," he said. "Stay right there." He ran upstairs to the bathroom and rummaged in the medicine chest for alcohol, cotton, and a Band-Aid. When he came back down she was leaning against the refrigerator with her eyes closed, still holding her hand. He took the hand and dabbed at her thumb with the cotton. The bleeding had stopped. He squeezed it to see how deep the wound was and a single drop of blood welled up, trembling and bright, and fell to the floor. Over the thumb she stared at him accusingly. "It's shallow," he said. "Tomorrow you won't even know it's there." He hoped that she appreciated how quickly he had come to her aid. He'd acted out of concern for her, with no thought of getting anything in return, but now the thought occurred to him that it would be a nice gesture on her part not to start up that conversation again, as he was tired of it. "I'll finish up here," he said. "You go and relax."

"That's okay," she said. "I'll dry."

He began to wash the silverware again, giving a lot of attention to the forks.

"So," she said, "you wouldn't have married me if I'd been black."

"For Christ's sake, Ann!"

"Well, that's what you said, didn't you?"

"No, I did not. The whole question is ridiculous. If you had been black we probably wouldn't even have met. You would have had your friends and I would have had mine. The only black girl I ever really knew was my partner in the debating club, and I was already going out with you by then."

"But if we had met, and I'd been black?"

"Then you probably would have been going out with a black guy." He picked up the rinsing nozzle and sprayed the silverware. The water was so hot that the metal darkened to pale blue, then turned silver again.

"Let's say I wasn't," she said. "Let's say I am black and unattached and we meet and fall in love."

He glanced over at her. She was watching him and her eyes were bright. "Look," he said, taking a reasonable tone, "this is stupid. If you were black you wouldn't be you." As he said this he realized it was absolutely true. There was no possible way of arguing with the fact that she would not be herself if she were black. So he said it again: "If you were black you wouldn't be you."

"I know," she said, "but let's just say."

He took a deep breath. He had won the argument but he still felt cornered. "Say what?" he asked.

"That I'm black, but still me, and we fall in love. Will you marry me?"

He thought about it.

"Well?" she said, and stepped close to him. Her eyes were even brighter. "Will you marry me?"

"I'm thinking," he said.

"You won't, I can tell. You're going to say no."

"Let's not move too fast on this," he said. "There are lots of things to consider. We don't want to do something we would regret for the rest of our lives."

"No more considering. Yes or no."

"Since you put it that way —"

"Yes or no."

"Jesus, Ann. All right. No."

She said, "Thank you," and walked from the kitchen

into the living room. A moment later he heard her turning the pages of a magazine. He knew that she was too angry to be actually reading it, but she didn't snap through the pages the way he would have done. She turned them slowly, as if she were studying every word. She was demonstrating her indifference to him, and it had the effect he knew she wanted it to have. It hurt him.

He had no choice but to demonstrate his indifference to her. Quietly, thoroughly, he washed the rest of the dishes. Then he dried them and put them away. He wiped the counters and the stove and scoured the linoleum where the drop of blood had fallen. While he was at it, he decided, he might as well mop the whole floor. When he was done the kitchen looked new, the way it looked when they were first shown the house, before they had ever lived here.

He picked up the garbage pail and went outside. The night was clear and he could see a few stars to the west, where the lights of the town didn't blur them out. On El Camino the traffic was steady and light, peaceful as a river. He felt ashamed that he had let his wife get him into a fight. In another thirty years or so they would both be dead. What would all that stuff matter then? He thought of the years they had spent together and how close they were and how well they knew each other, and his throat tightened so that he could hardly breathe. His face and neck began to tingle. Warmth flooded his chest. He stood there for a while, enjoying these sensations, then picked up the pail and went out the back gate.

The two mutts from down the street had pulled over the garbage can again. One of them was rolling around on his back and the other had something in her mouth.

Growling, she tossed it into the air, leaped up and caught it, growled again and whipped her head from side to side. When they saw him coming they trotted away with short, mincing steps. Normally he would heave rocks at them, but this time he let them go.

The house was dark when he came back inside. She was in the bathroom. He stood outside the door and called her name. He heard bottles clinking, but she didn't answer him. "Ann, I'm really sorry," he said. "I'll make it up to you, I promise."

"How?" she asked.

He wasn't expecting this. But from a sound in her voice, a level and definite note that was strange to him, he knew that he had to come up with the right answer. He leaned against the door. "I'll marry you," he whispered.

"We'll see," she said. "Go on to bed. I'll be out in a minute."

He undressed and got under the covers. Finally he heard the bathroom door open and close.

"Turn off the light," she said from the hallway.

"What?"

"Turn off the light."

He reached over and pulled the chain on the bedside lamp. The room went dark. "All right," he said. He lay there, but nothing happened. "All right," he said again. Then he heard a movement across the room. He sat up but he couldn't see a thing. The room was silent. His heart pounded the way it had on their first night together, the way it still did when he woke at a noise in the darkness and waited to hear it again — the sound of someone moving through the house, a stranger.

THE POOR ARE
ALWAYS WITH US

The trouble with owning a Porsche is that there's always some little thing wrong with it. This time it was a sticky brake pedal. Russell had planned a trip for Easter weekend, so he left work early on Friday afternoon and drove up to Menlo Park to have Bruno, his mechanic, take a look at the car. Bruno was an Austrian. The wall behind his desk was covered with diplomas, most written in German, congratulating him on his completion of different courses in Porsche technology. Bruno's office overlooked the bay where he and his assistant worked on the cars, both of them wearing starched white smocks and wielding tools that glittered like surgical instruments.

When Russell pulled into the garage, Bruno was alone. He looked up, waved, and bent back down under the hood of a vintage green Speedster. Russell walked around the Speedster a couple of times, then watched over Bruno's shoulder as Bruno traced the wiring with a flashlight whose thin silver beam looked as solid as a knitting needle.

"So?" Bruno asked. After Russell described the trouble he was having, Bruno grunted and said, "Sure sure. No sweat, old bean." He said that he would get to it as soon as he was done with the Speedster — forty-five minutes, maybe an hour. Russell could wait or pick it up on Monday.

Russell told him he would wait.

There were two men in Bruno's office. They glanced

at Russell when he came in, then went on talking above the noise of a radio on Bruno's desk that was playing music from the 1950s. Russell couldn't help listening to them. They were friends; he could tell that by the way they kept insulting each other. They never let up, especially the bigger of the two, a black guy who wore sunglasses and a safari jacket and popped his knuckles steadily. Whenever the white guy got off a good line the black guy would grin and shake his head and get off a better one. Twice Russell laughed out loud, and after the second time the white guy turned and stared at him. He had red-rimmed eyes that bulged as if some pressure inside him were forcing them out. His skin was tight-looking, drawn so severely over the bones of his face that even now, unsmiling as he was, his teeth showed. He stared at Russell and said, "Little pitchers have big ears."

Russell looked down at the rug. He tried to mind his own business after that, until the two men began to talk about someone from Russell's company who had recently been arrested for selling information on a new computer to the Japanese. Russell had met the man once, and from what these two fellows were saying he gathered that they had both worked with him at Hewlett-Packard a few years back. Russell knew he should keep his mouth shut, but he decided to say something. He had followed the case and had strong opinions about it. Mostly, though, he just wanted to join in the conversation.

"We all got our price," the black guy was saying. "Shit, they'd put every one of us in stir if they could read our minds for an hour. Any hour," he added.

"As if everybody else in this town isn't doing something just as bad," the white guy said. "As bad or worse. Bunch of piglets. They're just burned up because he got to the trough before they did."

"I see it differently," Russell said. "I think they should lock him up and throw away the key. He sold out the people who worked with him and trusted him. He sold out his team. As far as I'm concerned he's a complete write-off."

The white guy fixed his eyes on Russell and said, "Groves, who is this weenie?"

"Now, now," Groves said.

"I swear to God," the white guy said. He pushed himself out of his chair and went to the window overlooking the garage, coming down hard on the heels of his boots as he walked. He stood there, hands clenched into fists, and when he turned away Russell saw that his upper teeth were almost entirely exposed. He squinted at Russell. "A complete write-off," he said. "How old are you, anyway?"

Groves popped a knuckle. "Easy does it," he said. "Lighten up there, Dave."

Dave, Russell thought. He didn't know any Daves, but this one had something against him. "Twenty-two," he said, adding a year.

"Well then, I guess you know it all. From the lofty perspective of your twenty-two years."

"I don't know it all," Russell said. "I know the difference between right and wrong, though." *I hardly ever talk like this*, Russell wanted to add. *You should hear me with my friends back home.*

The pants Dave wore looked too small for him, and now he made them look even smaller by jamming his hands into the back pockets. "Go away," he said to Russell. "Go away and come back later, okay?"

"Easy does it," Groves said again. He put a small silver

bong on Bruno's desk and began to stuff it with brown marijuana from a sandwich bag. "Peace pipe," he said. He lit up and passed the bong to Russell. Russell took a hit and held it out to Dave, but Dave kept his hands in his pockets. Russell put the bong back down on Bruno's desk. He wished that he had refused it too.

"While we're on the subject," Dave said, "is there anybody else you want to write off?"

"Unbelievable," Groves said, turning up the volume on the radio. " 'Runaround Sue.' Man, I haven't heard 'Runaround Sue' in about eighty years."

Dave looked gloomily out the window. "Is that your Targa?" he asked. Without waiting for Russell to answer, he said, "How do you rate a Targa? Graduation present from Pop?"

"I bought it myself," Russell said.

Dave asked Russell where he worked, and when Russell told him, he said, "That outfit. Nothing but Jap spies and boy wonders. I swear to God they'll be hiring them out of first grade next."

"I do dearly love a Porsche," Groves said. "There isn't anything I wouldn't do to get me a Porsche."

Dave said, "Why don't you buy one?"

"Ask my wife."

"Which wife?"

"You see my problem," Groves said. He fired up the bong again and offered it to Russell. "Go on, child, go on," he insisted when Russell shook his head, and kept pushing it at him until Russell took another hit. Russell held the smoke in his mouth, then blew it out and said, "Gracias. That's righteous weed."

"Righteous!" Dave said. He grinned at Groves, who bent

over and made a sound like air escaping from a balloon. Groves began to drum his feet on the floor. "Gracias!" Dave said, and Groves threw his head back and howled.

Bruno came into the office carrying a clipboard. "You chaps," he said. "Always laughing." He sat down at the desk and started punching away at a pocket calculator.

Groves said, "Oh Lord. Lord Lord Lord." He pushed up his sunglasses and rubbed his eyes.

Bruno tore a sheet off the clipboard. "Seventy-two fifty," he said to Dave.

"Catch you tomorrow," Dave said.

"Better now," Bruno told him. "Tomorrow something bad might happen."

Dave slowly counted out the money. He was putting his wallet in his pocket when Groves pointed at him and said, "Name that tune!"

" 'Turn Me Loose,' " Dave said. "Kookie Byrnes. Nineteen fifty-eight."

"Fabian," Russell said.

"What do *you* know?" Dave said. "You weren't even born when this song came out."

Russell said, "It's Fabian. I'll bet you anything. I'll bet you my car."

Dave studied Russell for a moment. "Boy, you do bad things to me, you know that? Okay," he said. "My Speedster against your Targa."

Russell turned to Bruno. "You heard that."

"Get your papers," Bruno said.

Russell had his in his wallet. Dave's were in the glove compartment of the Speedster. While he was down in the garage getting them, Groves stood up and began to walk around the office. "I don't fucking believe this," he said.

Dave came back and handed the papers to Bruno, and they all waited for the song to end. But when it ended, two more songs played back to back: "My Prayer" and "Duke of Earl." Then the dee-jay came on and gave the names of the recording artists.

"Nuts," Dave said. Then, to Russell, "You little weenie."

The whole thing caught Bruno on his funnybone. He laughed until tears came to his eyes. "You crazy chaps," he said. "You crazy, crazy chaps."

Russell agreed to let Dave bring the car over to his apartment later that afternoon. He had legal title now; if Dave didn't show up, Russell could have him arrested for grand theft auto. Bruno was the one who made this point. Still laughing, Bruno got his camera out of the desk and took several pictures of the Speedster to keep as souvenirs of the event.

Russell waited alone in the office while Bruno put the Targa right; then he drove home and ate a sandwich beside the pool in the courtyard of his apartment building. He had the place to himself. All the other tenants were still at work, and none of them had children. Some owned dogs, but they'd been trained not to bark, so the courtyard was quiet except for the sigh of traffic from Page Mill Road and the tick of palm fronds above the chair where Russell sat.

He hated to think of giving the Speedster back. He wanted to keep it, and he could give himself reasons for keeping it, reasons that made sense. But all of them sounded like lies to Russell — the kind of lies you tell yourself when you already know the truth. The truth was that he'd been certain Fabian was the singer, and certain that Dave would take his bet. He had smoked marijuana in the middle of the afternoon like some kind of junior-high dropout, and lied about his age, and generally made a fool of himself. Then, because his feelings were hurt, he had goaded a man into gambling away his car.

That was how the truth looked to Russell, and it had nothing to do with his dream of being a magnanimous person, openhearted and fair. Of course, not everyone would see it this way. Russell knew that most people would think he was being fussy.

Russell lived alone now, but when he first arrived in town he had roomed with a fellow from his company, an MIT graduate whose ambition was to make a bundle in a hurry, invest it, and then become a composer. He wrote moody violin pieces, which he sometimes played for Russell. Russell thought that they sounded great and that his roommate was a genius. But his roommate was also a swinger. He had girls in the apartment every weekend and sometimes even during the week, different girls, and one night he and Russell got into an argument about it. Russell hadn't said anything up to then but his roommate knew that he disapproved. He wanted to know why. Russell told him that it seemed cheap. His roommate said, "You're completely uptight, that's your problem," and walked away, but he ran back a moment later yelling that nobody, but nobody, called him cheap and got away with it. He waved his long white hands in Russell's face and said, "How would you like a knuckle sandwich?" Russell apologized, and apologized again the next morning, and after that the two of them lived together on terms so polite that they would excuse themselves after coughing. Russell understood that his roommate had written him off.

Russell moved out at the end of the month. For a long

time afterwards, until he got used to living alone, he made up conversations with his old roommate in which he laid bare his soul, and was understood and forgiven. "Listen," Russell would say, "I know you think I'm uptight because I don't sleep around or do many drugs or party a lot. But I'm not uptight, I'm really not. I just don't want to end up like Teddy Wells. I don't want to end up fifty years old and getting my sixth divorce and wearing gold chains and putting half my salary up my nose and collecting erotic art and cruising El Camino for teen-agers."

And Russell's roommate would answer, "I never looked at it that way before, but I see what you mean and you're absolutely right."

Russell just wanted to keep his bearings, that was all. It was easy to lose your bearings when you were three thousand miles from home and making more money than you needed, almost twice as much as your own father made after thirty years of teaching high school math. "I'm just getting started," Russell would say. "I'm doing the best I can!"

And his roommate would answer, "Of course. Of course."

Dave brought the Speedster by at five-thirty, half an hour later than he'd promised. Russell was waiting outside the apartment building when Dave drove up. A dark-haired woman in an old station wagon pulled in behind the Speedster and sat there with the engine running. Dave rolled his window down. "Did you call the heat yet?" he asked.

"I knew you'd come," Russell said. He smiled, but Dave did not smile back.

"That's funny," Dave said. "A throw-away-the-key guy like you, I figured you'd have my picture in the post office by now." He got out and closed the door gently. "Here," he said, and tossed Russell the keys. "What are you going to do with it? Sell it?" He looked at the car, then back at Russell.

"No," Russell said. "Listen —"

Dave said, "You listen." He crossed the strip of grass to the sidewalk where Russell stood. Russell felt the man's hatred and took a step backwards. The woman in the station wagon revved the engine. Dave stopped and looked back at her, then put his hands in his pockets as he had done earlier that day. Russell understood the gesture now: it was what Dave did with his hands to keep them from doing something else.

"I wish this hadn't happened," Russell said.

Though Dave was a couple of inches shorter than Russell, he seemed to be examining him from a height. "You're nothing special," he said. "You might think you have ideas, but you don't. No one has had an actual idea in this business for about five years. You want to know how I got the Speedster?" When Russell didn't answer, he said: "I'll tell you. They gave it to me for an idea I had, actually a lot of ideas put together. They just handed me the keys and told me where it was parked and that was that. No speeches or anything. No plaque. Everything was understood."

The woman in the station wagon revved the engine again. Dave ignored her. He said, "You little snots think you're on the cutting edge but all you're doing is just sweeping up, collecting our stuff. The work's been done. You're just a bunch of janitors."

"That's not true," Russell said.

"You're a janitor," Dave repeated. "No way in hell do you rate a car like that. A car like that is completely out of your class." He took a quarter from his pocket and said, "Flip me for it."

"Flip you? Flip you for what?"

Dave looked down the street where the woman sat watching them. "The wagon," he said.

"Come on," Russell said. "What kind of deal is that?"

Dave flipped the quarter. "Call it."

"This is baloney," Russell said. Then, because he was afraid of Dave and wanted to be done with him, he said, "What the hell. All right. Tails."

"Tails it is," Dave said, and threw the coin into Russell's face. It struck him below the eye and fell to the sidewalk. Dave walked back to the station wagon. He knocked on the window, and when the woman rolled it down he reached past her, turned off the engine, and dropped the keys into the gutter.

"Hey," she said.

"Get out," Dave told her, and held the door open until she obeyed him. She was thin and pale. She had liquid brown eyes like a deer's eyes, and like a deer she looked restlessly around her as if unsure of everything.

"I'll send Groves over with the papers," Dave said. He turned and started down the street toward Page Mill Road. The woman watched him walk away, then looked at Russell.

"I'm sorry," he said. "It wasn't my idea."

"Oh no," she said. "Wait a minute. Dave!" she called, but Dave kept walking and didn't look back. "Don't go anywhere," she told Russell. "Just wait here, okay?" She took a couple of steps and gave a loud scream. Then she broke into a run, stopping once to scream again — no words, only the pure sound rising between the tiled rooftops into the cloudless blue sky.

Russell ate dinner at a Chinese place near the freeway. When he got home, he found Groves leaning back in one of the chairs by the side of the pool. The woman who managed the building was sitting beside him. She was a widow from Michigan. The other tenants complained about her because she was snoopy and enforced all the rules. In the eight months since Russell moved in he had never seen her smile, but when he stepped into the courtyard she was laughing.

"That's gospel," Groves said. "I swear."

She laughed again.

It was dark but Groves still had his sunglasses on. His hands were folded behind his head. When he saw Russell, he pointed one foot at him and said, "Here come de champ."

"Sorry I made you wait," Russell said. "I didn't know you'd be coming tonight."

"See?" Groves said. "I'm no perpetrator." He pushed himself up from the chair and said to Russell, "Emma here thought I was a perpetrator."

"No I didn't!" she said.

Groves laughed. "That's cool. Everybody gets one mistake." He clapped his hand on Russell's shoulder. "Champ, we got to talk."

Russell led Groves up the stairs and along the walkway to his apartment. Groves followed him inside and looked around. "What's this number?" he asked. "You in training to be a monk or something?"

"I just moved in a while ago," Russell said.

"No pictures, no sounds, no box," Groves went on. "No nothing. You sure you live here?" He took an envelope from his pocket and dropped it on the counter that divided the living room from the kitchen. "Candygram from Dave," he said. "Crazy Dave. Champ, we got a problem." Groves began to pace the small room, deliberately at first, then faster and faster, wheeling like a cat in a cage, the unbuckled straps of his safari jacket swinging at his sides. "We got a priority situation here," he said, "because you just got yourself all tied up in something you don't understand, and what you don't understand is my man Dave isn't in *no* condition to go laying off his automobiles at this point in time. He isn't what we say *competent*, you dig? What we're talking about here is some serious post-Vietnam shit. I mean serious head problems."

Without slowing down, Groves lit a cigarette. Then he went on talking, waving his hands and scattering ash onto the carpet. "What we've got here is a disturbed veteran. We've got a man who's been on the big march through the valley of the shadow of death, you follow me? I'm talking about Khe Sanh, champ. The Pit. Here's how it went down. Dave's company is sitting out on the perimeter or whatever and the Cong come pouring over, you with me? There's mortars going off and all that shit and rifles and whatever, and a whole bunch of Dave's friends, I mean his special dudes, get shot up. I mean they're hanging out there on the wire and so on. Now my man Dave, he's been hit too but what he does, he crawls out there anyway and drags his buddies in. All of them. Even the dead ones. And all the time old Charlie Cong is just *raining* on him. I mean he's got holes in places you never even *heard* of."

Groves shook his head. "Two years in the hospital,

champ. Two years all wrapped up like some kind of horror movie, and then what do they do? They give him the Congressional Medal of Honor and say, Sayonara, sucker. He don't think straight anymore that's not their problem, right?"

Groves walked around the counter. He ran water on the butt of his cigarette and dropped it in the sink. "What I'm saying is, you got any self-respect you don't go ripping no automobiles off of no disturbed veterans with the Congressional fucking Medal of Honor. That's what I'm saying here tonight."

Groves leaned forward against the counter and smiled at Russell. "Child," he said, "why don't you just give the man his cars back?"

"My name is Russell. And I don't believe that story. I don't believe that Dave was even in Vietnam."

"Damn!" Groves said. "Where's your imagination?" He took his sunglasses off, laid them on the counter, and began to rub his eyes in a way that made Russell think they were causing him pain — slowly, with his fingertips. "I don't know," he said. "All right. Let's take it again. We're talking about Dave."

Russell nodded.

"Dave's a good head," Groves went on. "I admit he's not that great with the general public, but he's okay. Lots of smarts, too. I mean, I'm smart, but Dave is *smart*. It used to be just about everybody in town wanted a piece of him. Dave was centerfold material for a while there, but nowadays things just keep messing up on him. It's like the well went dry. Happens to plenty of people. It could happen to you. I mean you might be coming up with sweet stuff today but there's no law says it's got to be there tomorrow, and just maybe it won't be. You ought to think about that."

"I do," Russell said.

"Now his wife's gone and left him. No concern of yours, but Lord, what a business."

"I tried to give the car back to him," Russell said. "He didn't give me a chance. He wouldn't even let me talk."

Groves laughed.

"It wasn't funny," Russell said. "I've had the willies all night. He really scared me, Groves. That's why I can't give him the car back now. I'd always wonder if I did it just because I was afraid of him. I wouldn't ever feel right about it."

Groves said, "Russell, I never saw no eighty-year-old man looked like you before."

"What I'm going to do is give the Speedster to you," Russell said. "Then you can give it to Dave. That's something I can live with. But I'm going to keep the station wagon," Russell added. "I won that fair and square."

"Well, now," Groves said. He seemed about to go on, but finally he just shook his head and looked down at the counter.

Russell had the papers in his pocket. He spread them out. "How do I write your name?" he asked.

"Just like it sounds. Groves. Tom Groves." As Russell took the cap from his pen, Groves said, in a quiet voice, "Make that Thomas B. Groves, Junior."

Russell never saw Groves again, but from time to time he felt a coldness on his back and looked around to find Dave watching him from another line in the market where he shopped, or through the window of the bank where he

kept his money. Dave never said anything, never accused,
but Russell began to think that he was being followed and
that a showdown was soon to come. He tried to prepare
himself for it. There were times at night and even at work
when Russell made angry faces, and shook his head, and
glared at things without seeing them as he rehearsed again
and again the proofs of his own decency. This went on for
almost a year.

Then, in April, he saw Dave on El Camino. Russell had
parked in the customer lot of a liquor store and was waiting for his date to come out with some wine for a party
they were going to. He was sitting there, watching the
cars go by, when he caught sight of Dave standing on the
curb across the road. Russell felt sure that Dave had not
seen him, because Dave was giving all his attention to the
traffic. He swung his head back and forth as the cars rushed
past him, looking, Russell supposed, for a chance to cross.
Sometimes the line of cars heading north would thin out,
and sometimes the line heading south, but never both together. There was no light nearby and no pedestrian cross-
ing, because on El Camino there were no pedestrians. You
never saw anyone on foot.

Dave went on waiting for a break to come. Twice he
stepped into the road as if to test his luck, but both times
he changed his mind and turned back. Russell watched
for Dave to bare his teeth and scream and shake his fists.
Nothing like this happened. He stood there and waited
for his chance, leaning into the road a little as he looked
each way. His face was calm. He accepted this situation,
saw nothing outrageous in it — nothing to make him go
home and come back with a gun and shoot every driver
on the road.

Finally Dave spotted an opening and made a run for it. He moved heavily but for all he was worth, knees flying high, arms flailing the air, and Russell's heart went out to the man. At that moment he would have given Dave everything he had — his money, his car, his job, everything — but what was the point? It didn't make sense trying to help Dave, because Dave couldn't be helped. Whatever Russell gave him he would lose. It just wasn't in the cards for him to have anything.

When Dave reached the curb he stopped and caught his breath. Then he started south in the direction of Mountain View. Russell watched him walk past the parking lot, watched him until he disappeared from sight. The low sun burned in the windows of a motel down the street. Above the motel rooftop, against the blue sky, hung a faint white haze like the haze of chalk dust on the blue suit Russell's father wore to school. Blurred shapes of cars flashed back and forth. Russell felt a little lost, and thought, *I'm on El Camino*. He was on El Camino. Just a short drive down the road some people were having a party, and he was on his way there.

SISTER

There was a park at the bottom of the hill. Now that the leaves were down Marty could see the exercise stations and part of a tennis court from her kitchen window, through a web of black branches. She took another doughnut from the box on the table and ate it slowly, watching the people at the exercise stations: two men and a woman. The woman was doing leg-raises. The men were just standing there. Though the day was cold one of the men had taken his shirt off, and even from this distance Marty was struck by the deep brown color of his skin. You hardly ever saw great tans like that on people around here, not even in summer. He had come from somewhere else.

She went into the bedroom and put on a running suit and an old pair of Adidas. The seams were giving out but her other pair was new and their whiteness made her feet look big. She took off her glasses and put her contacts in. Tears welled up under the lenses. For a few moments she lost her image in the mirror; then it returned and she saw the excitement in her face, the eagerness. *Whoa*, she thought. She sat there for a while, feeling the steady thump of the stereo in the apartment overhead. Then she rolled a joint and stuck it in the pocket of her sweatshirt.

A dog barked at Marty as she walked down the hallway. It barked at her every time she passed its door and it always took her by surprise, leaving her fluttery and breathless. The dog was a big shepherd whose owners were gone all the time. She could hear its feet scrabbling and see its nose pushed under the door. "Easy," she said, "easy there," but it kept trying to get at her, and Marty heard it barking all the way down the corridor until she reached the door and stepped outside.

It was late afternoon and cold, so cold she could see her breath. As always on Sunday the street was dead quiet, except for the skittering of leaves on the sidewalk as the breeze swept through them and ruffled the cold-looking pools of water from last night's rain. With the trees bare, the sky seemed vast. Two dark clouds drifted overhead, and in the far distance an angle of geese flew across the sky. Honkers, her brother called them. Right now he and his buddies would be banging away at them from one of the marshes outside town. By nightfall they'd all be drunk. She smiled, thinking of that.

Marty did a couple of knee-bends and headed toward the park, forcing herself to walk against the urge she felt to run. She considered taking a couple of hits off the joint in her pocket but decided against it. She didn't want to lose her edge.

The woman she'd seen at the exercise station was gone, but the two men were still there. Marty held back for a while, did a few more knee-bends and watched some boys playing football on the field behind the tennis courts. They couldn't have been more than ten or eleven but they moved like men, hunching up their shoulders and shaking their wrists as they jogged back to the huddle, grunting when they came off the line as if their bodies were big and weighty. You could tell that in their heads they had a whole stadium of people watching them. It tickled her.

Marty watched them run several plays, then she walked over to the exercise stations.

When she got there she had a shock. Marty recognized one of the men, and she was so afraid he would recognize her that she almost turned around and went home. He was a regular at the Kon-Tiki. A few weeks earlier he had taken notice of Marty and they'd matched daiquiris for a couple of hours and things looked pretty good. Then she went out to the car to get this book she'd been describing to him, a book about Edgar Cayce and reincarnation, and when she got back he was sitting on the other side of the room with someone else. He hadn't left anything for the drinks, so she got stuck with the bar bill. And her lighter was missing. The man's name was Jack. When she saw him leaning against the chin-up station she didn't know what to do. She wanted to vanish right into the ground.

But he seemed not to remember her. In fact, he was the one who said hello. "Hey there," he said.

She smiled at him. Then she looked at the tan one and said, "Hi."

He didn't answer. His eyes moved over her for a moment, and he looked away. He'd put on a warm-up jacket with a hood but left the zipper open nearly to his waist. His chest was covered with little curls of glistening golden hair. The other one, Jack, had on faded army fatigues with dark patches where the insignia had been removed. He needed a shave. He was holding a quart bottle of beer.

The two men had been talking when she walked up but now they were silent. Marty felt them watching her as she did her stretches. They had been talking about sex, she was sure of that. What they'd been saying was still in the air somehow, with the ripe smell of wet leaves and the rain-soaked earth. She took a deep breath.

Then she said, "You didn't get that tan around here." She kept rocking back and forth on her knuckles but looked up at him.

"You bet your buns I didn't," he said. "The only thing you get around here is arthritis." He pulled the zipper of his jacket up and down. "Hawaii. Waikiki Beach."

"Waikiki," Jack said. "Bikini-watching capital of the world."

"Brother, you speak true," the tan one said. "They've got this special breed over there that they raise just to walk back and forth in front of you. They ought to parachute about fifty of them into Russia. Those old farts in the Kremlin would go out of their skulls. We could just walk in and take the place over."

"They could drop a couple on this place while they're at it," Jack said.

"Amen." The tan one nodded. "Make it four — two apiece."

"Aloha," Marty said. She rolled over on her back and raised her feet a few inches off the ground. She held them there for a moment, then lowered them. "That's all the Hawaiian I know," she said. "Aloha and Maui Zowie. They grow some killer weed over there."

"For sure," the tan one said. "It's God's country, sister, and that's a fact."

Jack walked up closer. "I know you from somewhere," he said.

Oh no, Marty thought. She smiled at him. "Maybe," she said. "What's your name?"

"Bill," he said.

Right, Marty wanted to say. *You bet, Jack.*

Jack looked down at her. "What's yours?"

She raised her feet again. "Elizabeth."

"Elizabeth," he repeated, slowly, so that it struck Marty how beautiful the name was. Fairfield, she almost added, but she hesitated, and the moment passed.

"I guess not," he said.

She lowered her feet and sat up. "A lot of people look like me."

He nodded.

Just then something flew past Marty's head. She jerked to one side and threw her hands up in front of her face. She gave a shudder and looked around. "Jesus," she said.

"Sorry!" someone shouted.

"Goddam Frisbees," Jack said.

"It's all right," Marty told him, and waved at the man who'd thrown it. She turned and waved again at another man some distance behind her, who was wiping the Frisbee on his shirt. He waved back.

"Frisbee freaks," Jack said. "I'm sick of them." He lifted the bottle and drank from it, then held it out to Marty. "Go on," he told her.

She took a swig. "There's more than beer in here," she said.

Jack shrugged.

"What's in here?" she asked.

"Secret formula," he answered. "Go for two. You're behind."

Marty looked at the bottle, then drank again and passed it to the other man. Even his fingers were brown. He wore a thick wedding band and a gold chain-link bracelet. She held on to the bottle for an extra moment, long enough for him to notice and give her a look; then she let go. The hood of his jacket fell back as he tilted his head to drink. Marty saw that he was nearly bald. He had parted his hair just above one ear and swept it sideways to cover the skin on top, which was even darker than the rest of him.

"What's your name?" she asked.

Jack answered for him. "His name is Jack," he said.

The tan one laughed. "Brother," he said, "you are too much."

"You aren't from around here," she said. "I would have seen you."

He shook his head. "I was running and I ended up here."

Jack said, "Don't hog the fuel, Jack," and made a drinking motion with his hand.

The tan one nodded. He took a long pull and wiped his mouth and passed the bottle to Jack.

Marty stood and brushed off her warm-ups. "Hawaii," she said. "I've always wanted to go to Hawaii. Just kick back for about three weeks. Check out the volcanoes. Do some mai tais."

"Get leis," Jack said.

All three of them laughed.

"Well," she said. She touched her toes a couple of times. Jack kept laughing.

"Hawaii's amazing," said the other man. "Anything goes."

"Stop talking about Hawaii," Jack told him. "It makes me cold."

"Me too," Marty said. She rubbed her hands together. "I'm always cold. When I come back, I just hope I come back as a native of some place warm. California, maybe."

"Right," Jack said. "Bitchin' Cal," but there was something in his voice that made her look over at him. He was studying her. She could tell that he was trying to place her again, trying to recall where he'd met her. She wished she hadn't made that remark about coming back. That was what had set him off. She wasn't even sure she actually believed in it — believed that she was going to return as a different entity later on, someone new and different. She had serious doubts, sometimes. But at other times she thought it had to be true; this couldn't be everything.

"So," she said, "do you guys know each other?"

Jack stared at her a moment longer, then nodded. "All our lives," he said.

The tan one shook his head and laughed. "Too much," he said.

"We're inseparable," Jack said. "Aren't we, Jack?"

The tan one laughed again.

"Is that right?" Marty asked him. "Are you inseparable?"

He pulled the zipper of his jacket up and down, hiding and then revealing the golden hairs on his chest, though not in a conscious way. His cheeks puffed out and his brow thickened just above his eyes, so that his face seemed heavier. Marty could see that he was thinking. He looked at her and said, "I guess we are. For the time being."

"That's fine," she said. "That's all right." That was all right, she thought. She could call Jill, Jill was always up for a party, and if Jill was out or had company then she'd think of something else. It would work out.

"Okay," she said, but before she could say anything else someone yelled "Heads up!" and they all looked around. The Frisbee was coming straight at them. Marty felt her body tighten. "Got it," she said, and balanced her-

self for the catch. Suddenly the breeze gusted and the
Frisbee seemed to stop cold, a quivering red line, and then
it jerked upwards and flew over their heads and past them.
She ran after it, one arm raised, gathering herself to jump,
but it stayed just out of reach and finally she gave up.

The Frisbee flew a short distance farther, then fell to the
sidewalk and skidded halfway across the street. Marty
scooped it up and flipped it back into the park. She stood
there, wanting to laugh but completely out of breath. Too
much weed, she thought. She put her hands on her knees
and rocked back and forth. It was quiet. Then, from up
the hill, she heard a low rumble that grew steadily louder,
and a few seconds later a big white car came around the
corner. Its tires squealed and then went silent as the car
slid through a long sheet of water lying in the road. It was
moving sideways in her direction. She watched it come.
The car cleared the water and the tires began to squeal
again but it kept sliding, and Marty saw the faces inside
getting bigger and bigger. There was a girl staring at her
from the front window. The girl's mouth was open, her
arms braced against the dashboard. Then the tires caught
and the car shot forward, so close that Marty could have
reached out and touched the girl's cheek as they went past.

The car fish-tailed down the street. It ran a stop sign at
the corner and turned left back up the hill, coughing out
bursts of black exhaust.

Marty turned toward the park and saw the two men
looking at her. They were looking at her as if they had
seen her naked, and that was how she felt — naked. She
had nearly been killed and now she was an embarrassment,
like someone in need. She wasn't welcome in the park.

Marty crossed the street and started up the hill toward

her apartment building. She felt as if she were floating, as if there were nothing to her. She passed a grey cat curled up on the hood of a car. There was smoke on the breeze and the smell of decay. It seemed to Marty that she drifted with the smoke through the yellow light, over the dull grass and the brown clumps of leaves. In the park behind her a boy called football signals, his voice perfectly distinct in the thin cold air.

She climbed the steps to the building but did not go inside. She knew that the dog would bark at her, and she didn't think she could handle that right now.

She sat on the steps. From somewhere nearby a bird cried out in a hoarse, ratcheting voice like chain being jerked through a pulley. Marty did some breathing exercises to get steady, to quiet the fluttering sensation in her shoulders and knees, but she could not calm herself. A few minutes ago she had nearly been killed and now there was nobody to talk to about it, to see how afraid she was and tell her not to worry, that it was over now. That she was still alive. That everything was going to be all right.

At this moment, sitting here, Marty understood that there was never going to be anyone to tell her these things. She had no idea why this should be so; it was just something she knew. There was no need for her to make a fool of herself again.

The sun was going down. Marty couldn't see it from where she sat, but the windows of the house across the street had turned crimson, and the breeze was colder. A broken kite flapped in a tree. Marty fingered the joint in her pocket but left it there; she felt empty and clean, and did not want to lose the feeling.

She watched the sky darken. Her brother and his

friends would be coming off the marsh about now, flushed with cold and drink, their dogs running ahead through the reeds and the tall grass. When they reach the car they'll compare birds and pass a bottle around, and after the bottle is empty they will head for the nearest bar. Do boilermakers. Stuff themselves with pickled eggs and jerky. Throw dice from a leather cup. And outside in the car the dogs will be waiting, ears pricked for the least sound, sometimes whimpering to themselves but mostly silent, tense, and still, watching the bright door the men have closed behind them.

SOLDIER'S
JOY

On Friday Hooper was named driver of the guard for the third night that week. He had recently been broken in rank again, this time from corporal to PFC, and the first sergeant had decided to keep Hooper's evenings busy so that he would not have leisure to brood. That was what the first sergeant told Hooper when Hooper came to the orderly room to complain.

"It's for your own good," the first sergeant said. "Not that I expect you to thank me." He moved the book he'd been reading to one side of his desk and leaned back. "Hooper, I have a theory about you," he said. "Want to hear it?"

"I'm all ears, Top," Hooper said.

The first sergeant put his boots up on the desk and stared out the window to his left. It was getting on toward five o'clock. Work details had begun to return from the rifle range and the post laundry and the brigade commander's house, where Hooper and several other men were excavating a swimming pool without aid of machinery. As the trucks let them out they gathered on the barracks steps and under the dead elm beside the mess hall, their voices a steady murmur in the orderly room where Hooper stood waiting for the first sergeant to speak.

"You resent me," the first sergeant said. "You think you should be sitting here. You don't know that's what you think because you've totally sublimated your resentment, but that's what it is all right, and that's why you and me are developing a definite conflict profile. It's like you have to keep fucking up to prove to yourself that you don't really care. That's my theory. You follow me?"

"Top, I'm way ahead of you," Hooper said. "That's night school talking."

The first sergeant continued to look out the window. "I don't know," he said. "I don't know what you're doing in my army. You've put your twenty years in. You could retire to Mexico and buy a peso factory. Live like a dictator. So what are you doing in my army, Hooper?"

Hooper looked down at the desk. He cleared his throat but said nothing.

"Give it some thought," the first sergeant said. He stood and walked Hooper to the door. "I'm not hostile," he said. "I'm prepared to be supportive. Just think nice thoughts about Mexico, okay? Okay, Hooper?"

Hooper called Mickey and told her he wouldn't be coming by that night after all. She reminded him that this was the third time in one week, and said that she wasn't getting any younger.

"What am I supposed to do?" Hooper asked. "Go AWOL?"

"I cried three times today," Mickey said. "I just broke down and cried, and you know what? I don't even know why. I just feel bad all the time anymore."

"What did you do last night?" Hooper asked. When Mickey didn't answer he said, "Did Briggs come over?"

"I've been inside all day," Mickey said. "Just sitting here. I'm going out of my tree." Then, in the same weary voice, she said, "Touch it, Hoop."

"I have to get going," Hooper said.

"Not yet. Wait. I'm going into the bedroom. I'm going to pick up the phone in there. Hang on, Hoop. Think of the bedroom. Think of me lying on the bed. Wait, baby."

There were men passing by the phone booth. Hooper watched them and tried not to think of Mickey's bedroom but now he could think of nothing else. Mickey's husband was a supply sergeant with a taste for quality. The walls of the bedroom were knotty pine he'd derailed en route to some colonel's office. The brass lamps beside the bed were made from howitzer casings. The sheets were parachute silk. Sometimes, lying on those sheets, Hooper thought of the men who had drifted to earth below them. He was no great lover, as the women he went with usually got around to telling him, but in Mickey's bedroom Hooper had turned in his saddest performances and always when he was most aware that everything around him was stolen. He wasn't exactly sure why he kept going back. It was just something he did, again and again.

"Okay," Mickey said. "I'm here."

"There's a guy waiting to use the phone," Hooper told her.

"Hoop, I'm on the bed. I'm taking off my shoes."

Hooper could see her perfectly. He lit a cigarette and opened the door of the booth to let the smoke out.

"Hoop?" she said.

"I told you, there's a guy waiting."

"Turn around then."

"You don't need me," Hooper said. "All you need is the telephone. Why don't you call Briggs? That's what you're going to do after I hang up."

"I probably will," she said. "Listen, Hoop, I'm not

really on the bed. I was just pulling your chain. I thought it would make me feel better but it didn't."

"I knew it," Hooper said. "You're watching the tube, right?"

"Somebody just won a saw," Mickey said.

"A saw?"

"Yeah, they drove up to this man's house and dumped a truckload of logs in his yard and gave him a chainsaw. This was his fantasy. You should see how happy he is, Hoop. I'd give anything to be that happy."

"Maybe I can swing by later tonight," Hooper said. "Just for a minute."

"I don't know," Mickey said. "Better give me a ring first."

After Mickey hung up Hooper tried to call his wife but there was no answer. He stood there and listened to the phone ringing. At last he put the receiver down and stepped outside the booth, just as they began to sound retreat over the company loudspeaker. With the men around him Hooper came to attention and saluted. The record was scratchy, but, as always, the music caused Hooper's mind to go abruptly and perfectly still. The stillness spread down through his body. He held his salute until the last note died away, then broke off smartly and walked down the street toward the mess hall.

The Officer of the Day was Captain King from Headquarters Company. Captain King had also been Officer of the Day on Monday and Tuesday nights, and Hooper was glad to see him again because Captain King was too lazy to do his own job or to make sure that the guards were doing theirs. He stayed in the guardhouse and left everything up to Hooper.

Captain King had grey hair and a long greyish face. He was a West Point graduate with twenty-eight years of service behind him, just trying to make it through another two years so he could retire at three-quarters pay. All his classmates were generals or at least bird colonels but he himself had been held back for good reasons, many of which he admitted to Hooper their first night together. It puzzled Hooper at first, this officer telling him about his failures to perform, his nervous breakdowns and Valium habit, but finally Hooper understood: Captain King regarded him, a PFC with twenty-one years' service, as a comrade in dereliction, a disaster like himself with no room left for judgment against anyone.

The evening was hot and muggy. Little black bats swooped overhead as Captain King made his way along the rank of men drawn up before the guardhouse steps. He objected to the alignment of someone's belt buckle. He asked questions about the chain of command but gave no sign as to whether the answers he received were right or wrong. He inspected a couple of rifles and pretended to find something amiss with each of them, though it was clear that he hardly knew one end from the other, and when he reached the last man in the line he began to deliver a speech. He said that he had never seen such sorry troops in his life. He asked how they expected to stand up to a determined enemy. On and on he went. Captain King had delivered the same speech on Monday and Tuesday, and when Hooper recognized it he lit another cigarette and sat down on the running board of the truck he'd been leaning against.

The sky was grey. It had a damp, heavy look and it felt heavy too, hanging close overhead, nervous with rumblings and small flashes in the distance. Just sitting there made

Hooper sweat. Beyond the guardhouse a stream of cars rushed along the road to Tacoma. From the officers' club farther up the road came the muffled beat of rock music, which was almost lost, like every other sound of the evening, in the purr of crickets that rose up everywhere and thickened the air like heat.

When Captain King had finished talking he turned the men over to Hooper for transportation to their posts. Two of them, both privates, were from Hooper's company and these he allowed to ride with him in the cab of the truck while everybody else slid around in back. One was a cook named Porchoff, known as Porkchop. The other was a radio operator named Trac who had managed to airlift himself out of Saigon during the fall of the city by hanging from the skids of a helicopter. That was the story Hooper had heard, anyway, and he had no reason to doubt it; he'd seen the slopes pull that trick plenty of times, though few of them were as young as Trac must have been then — eight or nine at the most. When Hooper tried to picture his son Wesley at the same age doing that, hanging over a burning city by his fingertips, he had to smile.

But Trac didn't talk about it. There was nothing about him to suggest his past except perhaps the deep, sickle-shaped scar above his right eye. To Hooper there was something familiar about this scar. One night, watching Trac play the video game in the company rec room, he was overcome with the certainty that he had seen Trac before somewhere — astride a water buffalo in some reeking paddy or running alongside Hooper's APC with a bunch of other kids all begging money, holding up melons or a bag full of weed or a starving monkey on a stick.

Though Hooper had the windows open, the cab of the

truck smelled strongly of aftershave. Hooper noticed that
Trac was wearing orange Walkman earphones under his
helmet liner. They were against regulations but Hooper
said nothing. As long as Trac had his ears plugged he
wouldn't be listening for trespassers and end up blowing
his rifle off at some squirrel cracking open an acorn. Of all
the guards only Porchoff and Trac would be carrying
ammunition, because they had been assigned to the bat-
talion communications center where there was a tie-in
terminal to the division mainframe computer. The theory
was that an intruder who knew his stuff could get his hands
on highly classified material. That was how it had been
explained to Hooper. Hooper thought it was a load of
crap. The Russians knew everything anyway.

Hooper let out the first two men at the PX and the next
two at the parking lot outside the main officers' club, where
lately there'd been several cars vandalized. As they pulled
away, Porchoff leaned over Trac and grabbed Hooper's
sleeve. "You used to be a corporal," he said.

Hooper shook Porchoff's hand loose. He said, "I'm driving a truck, in case you didn't notice."

"How come you got busted?"

"None of your business."

"I'm just asking," Porchoff said. "So what happened,
anyway?"

"Cool it, Porkchop," said Trac. "The man doesn't want
to talk about it, okay?"

"Cool it yourself, fuckface," Porchoff said. He looked
at Trac. "Was I addressing you?"

Trac said, "Man, you must've been eating some of your
own food."

"I don't believe I was addressing you," Porchoff said.

"In fact, I don't believe that you and me have been properly introduced. That's another thing I don't like about the army, the way people you haven't been introduced to feel perfectly free to get right into your face and unload whatever shit they've got in their brains. It happens all the time. But I never heard anyone say 'cool it' before. You're a real phrasemaker, fuckface."

"That's enough," Hooper said.

Porchoff leaned back and said, "That's enough," in a falsetto voice. A few moments later he started humming to himself.

Hooper dropped off the rest of the guards and turned up the hill toward the communications center. There were chokeberry bushes along the gravel drive, with white blossoms going grey in the dusky light. Gravel sprayed up under the tires and rattled against the floorboards of the truck. Porchoff stopped humming. "I've got a cramp," he said.

Hooper pulled up next to the gate and turned off the engine. He looked over at Porchoff. "Now what's your problem?" he said.

"I've got a cramp," Porchoff repeated.

"For Christ's sake," Hooper said. "Why didn't you say something before?"

"I did. I went on sick call but the doctor couldn't find it. It keeps moving around. It's here now." Porchoff touched his neck. "I swear to God."

"Keep track of it," Hooper told him. "You can go on sick call again in the morning."

"You don't believe me," Porchoff said.

The three of them got out of the truck. Hooper counted out the ammunition to Porchoff and Trac, and watched as they loaded their clips. "That ammo's strictly for show," he said. "Forget I even gave it to you. If you run into a problem, which you won't, use the phone in the guard shack. You can work out your own shifts." Hooper opened the gate and locked the two men inside. They stood watching him, faces in shadow, black rifle barrels poking over their shoulders. "Listen," Hooper said, "nobody's going to break in here, understand?"

Trac nodded. Porchoff just looked at him.

"Okay," Hooper said. "I'll drop by later. Me and the captain." Hooper knew that Captain King wasn't about to go anywhere, but Trac and Porchoff didn't know that. Hooper behaved better when he thought he was being watched and he supposed that the same was true of other people.

Hooper climbed back inside the truck and started the engine. He gave the V sign to the men at the gate. Trac gave the sign back and turned away. Porchoff didn't move. He stayed where he was, fingers laced through the wire. He looked about ready to cry. "Damn," Hooper said, and hit the gas. Gravel clattered in the wheel wells. When Hooper reached the main road a light rain began to fall, but it stopped before he'd even turned the wipers on.

Hooper and Captain King sat on adjacent bunks in the guardhouse, which was empty except for them and a bat that was flitting back and forth among the dim rafters. As on Monday and Tuesday nights, Captain King had brought along an ice chest filled with little bottles of Perrier water. From time to time he tried pressing one on Hooper, but Hooper declined. His refusals made Captain King apologetic. "It's not a class thing," Captain King said, looking at the bottle in his hand. "I don't drink this stuff because I went to the Point or anything like that." He leaned down and put the bottle between his bare feet. "I'm allergic to alcohol," he said. "Otherwise I'd probably be an alcoholic. Why not? I'm everything else." He smiled at Hooper.

Hooper lay back and clasped his hands behind his head and stared up at the mattress above him. "I'm not much of a drinker myself," he said. He knew that Captain King wanted him to explain why he refused the Perrier water but there was really no reason in particular. Hooper just didn't like the idea.

"I drank eggnog one Christmas when I was a kid and it almost killed me," Captain King said. "My arms and legs swelled up to twice their normal size. The doctors couldn't get my glasses off because my skin was all puffed up around them. You know the way a tree will grow around a rock. It was like that. A few months later I tried beer at some kid's graduation party and the same thing happened. Pretty strange, eh?"

"Yes sir," Hooper said.

"I used to think it was all for the best. I have an addictive personality and you can bet your bottom dollar I would have been a problem drinker. No question about it. But now I wonder. If I'd had one big weakness like that maybe I wouldn't have had all these little pissant weaknesses I ended up with. I know that sounds like bull-pucky, but look at Alexander the Great. Alexander the Great was a boozer. Did you know that?"

"No sir," Hooper said.

"Well, he was. Read your history. So was Churchill. Churchill drank a bottle of cognac a day. And of course Grant. You know what Lincoln said when someone complained about Grant's drinking?"

"Yes sir. I've heard the story."

"He said, 'Find out what brand he uses so I can ship a case to the rest of my generals.' Is that the way you heard it?"

"Yes sir."

Captain King nodded. "I'm all in," he said. He stretched out and assumed exactly the position Hooper was in. It made Hooper uncomfortable. He sat up and put his feet on the floor.

"Married?" Captain King asked.

"Yes sir."

"Kids?"

"Yes sir. One. Wesley."

"Oh my God, a boy," Captain King said. "They're nothing but trouble, take my word for it. They're programmed to hate you. It has to be like that, otherwise they'd spend their whole lives moping around the house, but just the same it's no fun when it starts. I have two and neither of them can stand me. Haven't been home in years. Breaks my heart. Of course I was a worse father than most. How old is your boy?"

"Sixteen or seventeen," Hooper said. He put his hands on his knees and looked at the floor. "Seventeen. He lives with my wife's sister in San Diego."

Captain King turned his head and looked at Hooper. "Sounds like you're not much of a dad yourself."

Hooper began to lace his boots up.

"I'm not criticizing," Captain King said. "At least you were smart enough to get someone else to do the job." He yawned. "I'm whipped," he said. "You need me for anything? You want me to make the rounds with you?"

"I'll take care of things, sir," Hooper said.

"Fair enough." Captain King closed his eyes. "If you need me just shout."

Hooper went outside and lit a cigarette. It was almost midnight, well past the time appointed for inspecting the guards. As he walked toward the truck mosquitoes droned around his head. A breeze was rustling the treetops, but on the ground the air was hot and still.

Hooper took his time making the rounds. He visited all the guards except Porchoff and Trac, and found everything in order. There were no problems. He started down the road toward the communications center, but when he reached the turn-off he kept his eyes dead ahead and drove past. Warm, fragrant air rushed into his face from the open window. The road ahead was empty. Hooper leaned back and mashed the accelerator. The engine roared. He was moving now, really moving, past darkened barracks and bare flagpoles and bushes whose flowers blazed up in the glare of the headlights. Hooper grinned. He felt no pleasure but he grinned and pushed the truck as hard as it would go.

Hooper slowed down when he left the post. He was AWOL now. Even if he couldn't find it in him to care much about that, he saw no point in calling attention to himself.

Drunk drivers were jerking their cars back and forth between lanes. Every half-mile or so a police car with flashing lights had someone stopped by the roadside. Other police cars sat idling behind billboards. Hooper stayed in the right lane and drove slowly until he reached his turn, then he gunned the engine again and raced down the pitted street that led to Mickey's house. He passed a bunch of kids sitting on the hood of a car with cans of beer in their hands. The car door was open and Hooper had to swerve to miss it. As he went by he heard a blast of music.

When he reached Mickey's block Hooper turned off
the engine. The truck coasted silently down the street, and
again Hooper became aware of the sound of crickets. He
stopped on the shoulder across from Mickey's house and
sat listening. The thick pulsing sound seemed to grow
louder every moment. Hooper drifted into memory, his
cigarette dangling unsmoked, burning its way toward his
fingers. At the same instant he felt the heat of the ember
against his skin Hooper was startled by another pain, the
pain of finding himself where he was. It left him breathless
for a moment. Then he roused himself and got out of the
truck.

The windows were dark. Mickey's Buick was parked in
the driveway beside another car that Hooper didn't recognize. It didn't belong to her husband and it didn't belong
to Briggs. Hooper glanced around at the other houses, then
walked across the street and ducked under the hanging
leaves of the willow tree in Mickey's front yard. He knelt
there, holding his breath to hear better, but there was no
sound but the sound of the crickets and the rushing of the
big air conditioner Mickey's husband had taken from a
helicopter hangar. Hooper saw no purpose in staying
under the tree, so he got up and walked over to the house.
He looked around again, then went into a crouch and
began to work his way along the wall. He rounded the
corner of the house and was starting up the side toward
Mickey's bedroom when a circle of light burst around his
head and a woman's voice said, "Thou shalt not commit
adultery."

Hooper closed his eyes. There was a long silence. Then
the woman said, "Come here."

She was standing in the driveway of the house next door.

When Hooper came up to her she stuck a pistol in his face and told him to raise his hands. "A soldier," she said, moving the beam of light up and down his uniform. "All right, put your hands down." She snapped the light off and stood watching Hooper in the flickering blue glow that came from the open door behind her. Hooper heard a dog bark twice and a man say, "Remember — nothing is too good for your dog. It's 'Ruff ruff' at the sign of the double R." The dog barked twice again.

"I want to know what you think you're doing," the woman said.

Hooper said, "I'm not exactly sure." He saw her more clearly now. She was thin and tall. She wore glasses with black frames, and she had on a white dress of the kind girls called "formals" when Hooper was in high school — tight around the waist and flaring stiffly at the hip, breasts held in hard-looking cups. Shadows darkened the hollows of her cheeks. Under the flounces of the dress her feet were big and bare.

"I know what you're doing," she said. She pointed the pistol, an Army .45, at Mickey's house. "You're sniffing around that whore over there."

Someone came to the door behind the woman. A deep voice called out, "Is it him?"

"Stay inside, Dads," the woman answered. "It's nobody."

"It's him!" the man shouted. "Don't let him talk you out of it again! Do it while you've got the chance, sweetie pie."

"What do you want with that whore?" the woman asked Hooper. Before he could answer, she said, "I could shoot you and nobody would say boo. I'm within my rights."

Hooper nodded.

"I don't see the attraction," she said. "But then I'm not a man." She made a laughing sound. "You know something? I almost did it. I almost shot you. I was that close, but then I saw the uniform." She shook her head. "Shame on you. Where is your pride?"

"Don't let him talk," said the man in the doorway. He came down the steps, a tall white-haired man in striped pajamas. "There you are, you sonofabitch," he said. "I'll dance on your grave."

"It isn't him, Dads," the woman said sadly. "It's someone else."

"So he says," the man snapped. He started down the driveway, hopping from foot to foot over the gravel. The woman handed him the flashlight and he turned it on in Hooper's face, then moved the beam slowly down to his boots. "Sweetie pie, it's a soldier," he said.

"I told you it wasn't him," the woman said.

"But this is a terrible mistake," the man said. "Sir, I'm at a loss for words."

"Forget it," Hooper told him. "No hard feelings."

"You are too kind," the man said. He reached out and shook Hooper's hand. "You're alive," he said. "That's what counts." He nodded toward the house. "Come have a drink."

"He has to go," the woman said. "He was looking for something and he found it."

"That's right," Hooper told him. "I was just on my way back to base."

The man gave a slight bow with his head. "To base with you, then. Good night, sir."

Hooper and the woman watched him make his way back to the house. When he was inside the woman turned to

Hooper and said, "If I told him what you were doing over there it would break his heart. But I won't tell him. There've been disappointments enough in his life already and God only knows what's next. He's got to have. something left." She drew herself up and gave Hooper a hard look. "Why are you still here?" she asked angrily. "Go back to your post."

Captain King was still asleep when Hooper returned to the guardhouse. His thumb was in his mouth and he made little noises as he sucked it. Hooper lay in the next bunk with his eyes open. He was still awake at four in the morning when the telephone began to ring.

It was Trac calling from the communications center. He said that Porchoff was threatening to shoot himself, and threatening to shoot Trac if Trac tried to stop him. "This dude is mental," Trac said. "You get me out of here and I mean now."

"We'll be right there," Hooper said. "Just give him lots of room. Don't try to grab his rifle or anything."

"Fat fucking chance," Trac said. "Man, you know what he called me? He called me a gook. I hope he wastes himself. I don't need no assholes with loaded guns declaring war on me, man."

"Just hang tight," Hooper told him. He hung up and went to wake Captain King, because this was a mess and he wanted it to be Captain King's mess and Captain King's balls that got busted if anything went wrong. He walked over to Captain King and stood looking down at him. Captain King's thumb had slipped out of his mouth but he was still making sucking noises and pursing up his lips. Hooper decided not to wake him after all. Captain King would probably refuse to come anyway, but if he did come he would screw things up for sure. Just the sight of him was enough to make somebody start shooting.

A light rain had begun to fall. The road was empty except for one jeep going the other way. Hooper waved at the two men in front as they went past, and they both waved back. Hooper felt a surge of friendliness toward them. He followed their lights in his mirror until they vanished behind him.

Hooper parked the truck halfway up the drive and walked the rest of the distance. The rain was falling harder now, tapping steadily on the shoulders of his poncho. Sweet, almost unbreathable smells rose from the earth. He walked slowly, gravel crunching under his boots. When he reached the gate a voice to his left said, "Shit, man, you took your time." Trac stepped out of the shadows and waited as Hooper tried to get the key into the lock. "Come on, man," Trac said. He knelt with his back to the fence and swung the barrel of his rifle from side to side.

"Got it," Hooper said. He took the lock off and Trac pushed open the gate. "The truck's down there," Hooper told him. "Just around the turn."

Trac stood close to Hooper, breathing quick shallow breaths and shifting from foot to foot. His face was dark under the hood of his glistening poncho. "You want this?" he asked. He held out his rifle.

Hooper looked at it. He shook his head. "Where's Porchoff?"

"Around back," Trac said. "There's some picnic benches out there."

"All right," Hooper said. "I'll take care of it. Wait in the truck."

"Shit, man, I feel like shit," Trac said. "I'll back you up, man."

"It's okay," Hooper told him. "I can handle it."

"I never cut out on anybody before," Trac said. He shifted back and forth.

"You aren't cutting out," Hooper said. "Nothing's going to happen."

Trac started down the drive. When he disappeared around the turn Hooper kept watching to make sure he didn't double back. A stiff breeze began to blow, shaking the trees, sending raindrops rattling down through the leaves. Thunder rumbled far away.

Hooper turned and walked through the gate into the compound. The forms of shrubs and pines were dark and indefinite in the slanting rain. Hooper followed the fence to the right, squinting into the shadows. When he saw Porchoff hunched over the picnic table he stopped and called out to him, "Hey, Porchoff! It's me — Hooper."

Porchoff raised his head.

"It's just me," Hooper said, following his own voice toward Porchoff, showing his empty hands. He saw the rifle lying on the table in front of Porchoff. "It's just me," he repeated, monotonously as he could. He stopped beside another picnic table ten feet or so from the one where Porchoff sat, and lowered himself onto the bench. He looked over at Porchoff. Neither of them spoke for a while. Then Hooper said, "Okay, Porchoff, let's talk about it. Trac tells me you've got some kind of attitude problem."

Porchoff didn't answer. Raindrops streamed down his helmet onto his shoulders and dripped steadily past his face. His uniform was soggy and dark, plastered to his skin. He stared at Hooper and said nothing. Now and then his shoulders jerked.

"Are you gay?" Hooper asked.

Porchoff shook his head.

"Well then, what? You on acid or something? You can tell me, Porchoff. It doesn't matter."

"I don't do drugs," Porchoff said. It was the first time he'd spoken. His voice was calm.

"Good," Hooper said. "I mean at least I know I'm talking to you and not to some fucking chemical. Now listen up, Porchoff — I don't want you turning that rifle on me. Understand?"

Porchoff looked down at the rifle, then back at Hooper. He said, "You leave me alone and I'll leave you alone."

"I've already had someone throw down on me once tonight," Hooper said. "I'd just as soon leave it at that." He reached under his poncho and took out his cigarette case. He held it up for Porchoff to see.

"I don't use tobacco," Porchoff said.

"Well I do," Hooper said. He shook out a cigarette and bent to light it. "Hey," he said. "All right. One match." He put the case back in his pocket and cupped the cigarette under the picnic table to keep it dry. The rain was falling lightly now in fine fitful gusts like spray. The clouds had gone the color of ash. Misty grey light was spreading through the sky. Hooper saw that Porchoff's shoulders twitched constantly now, and that his lips were blue and trembling. "Put your poncho on," Hooper told him.

Porchoff shook his head.

"You trying to catch pneumonia?" Hooper asked. He smiled at Porchoff. "Go ahead, boy. Put your poncho on."

Porchoff bent over and covered his face with his hands. Hooper realized that he was crying. He smoked his cigarette and waited for Porchoff to stop, but Porchoff kept crying and Hooper grew impatient. He said, "What's all this crap about you shooting yourself?"

Porchoff rubbed at his eyes with the heels of his hands. "Why shouldn't I?" he asked.

"Why shouldn't you? What do you mean, why shouldn't you?"

"Why shouldn't I shoot myself? Give me a reason."

"No. But I'll give you some advice," Hooper said. "You don't run around asking why shouldn't I shoot myself. That's decadent, Porchoff. Now do me a favor and put your poncho on."

Porchoff sat shivering for a moment. Then he took his poncho off his belt, unrolled it, and began to pull it over his head. Hooper considered making a grab for the rifle but held back. There was no need, he was home free now. People who were going to blow themselves away didn't come in out of the rain.

"You know what they call me?" Porchoff said.

"Who's they, Porchoff?"

"Everyone."

"No. What does everyone call you?"

"Porkchop. *Porkchop*."

"Come on," Hooper said. "What's the harm in that? Everyone gets called something."

"But that's my *name*," Porchoff said. "That's *me*. It's got so even when people use my real name I hear Porkchop. All I can think of is this big piece of meat. And that's what they're seeing, too. You can say they aren't, but I know they are."

Hooper recognized some truth in this, a lot of truth in fact, because when he himself said Porkchop that was what he saw: a porkchop.

"I hurt all the time," Porchoff said, "but no one believes me. Not even the doctors. You don't believe me either."

"I believe you," Hooper said.

Porchoff blinked. "Sure," he said.

"I believe you," Hooper repeated. He kept his eyes on the rifle. Porchoff wasn't going to waste himself but the rifle still made Hooper uncomfortable. He was about to ask Porchoff to give it to him but decided to wait a little while. The moment was wrong somehow. Hooper pushed back the hood of his poncho and took off his fatigue cap. He glanced up at the pale clouds.

"I don't have any buddies," Porchoff said.

"No wonder," Hooper said. "Calling people gooks, making threats. Let's face it, Porchoff, your personality needs some upgrading."

"But they won't give me a chance," Porchoff said. "All I ever do is cook food. I put it on their plates and they make some crack and walk on by. It's like I'm not even there. So what am I supposed to act like?"

Hooper was still gazing up at the clouds, feeling the soft rain on his face. Birds were starting to sing in the woods beyond the fence. He said, "I don't know, Porchoff. It's just part of this rut we're all in." Hooper lowered his head and looked over at Porchoff, who sat hunched inside his poncho, shaking as little tremors passed through him. "Any day now," Hooper said. "Everything's going to change."

"My dad was in the National Guard back in Ohio," Porchoff said. "He's always talking about the great experiences he and his buddies used to have, camping out and so on. Nothing like that ever happens to me." Porchoff looked down at the table, then looked up and said, "How about you? What was your best time?"

"My best time," Hooper said. The question made him

feel tired. He thought of telling Porchoff some sort of lie but the effort of making things up was beyond him and the memory Porchoff wanted was close at hand. For Hooper it was closer than the memory of home. In truth it was a kind of home. It was where he went to be back with his friends again, and his old self. It was where Hooper drifted when he was too low to care how much lower he'd be when he drifted back, and lost it all again. "Vietnam," he said.

Porchoff just looked at him.

"We didn't know it then," Hooper said. "We used to talk about how when we got back in the world we were going to do this and we were going to do that. Back in the world we were going to have it made. But ever since then it's been nothing but confusion." Hooper took the cigarette case from his pocket but didn't open it. He leaned forward on the table.

"Everything was clear," he said. "You learned what you had to know and you forgot the rest. All this chickenshit. This clutter. You didn't spend every living minute of the day thinking about your own sorry-ass little self. Am I getting laid enough. What's wrong with my kid. Should I insulate the fucking house. That's what does it to you, Porchoff. Thinking about yourself. That's what kills you in the end."

Porchoff had not moved. In the grey light Hooper could see Porchoff's fingers spread before him on the tabletop, white and still as if they had been drawn there in chalk. His face was the same color.

"You think you've got problems, Porchoff, but they wouldn't last five minutes in the field. There's nothing wrong with you that a little search-and-destroy wouldn't cure." Hooper paused, smiling to himself, already deep in the memory. He tried to bring it back for Porchoff, tried to put it into words so that Porchoff could see it too, the beauty of that life, the faith so deep that in time you were not separate men anymore, but part of each other.

But the words came hard. Hooper saw that Porchoff did not understand, and then he realized that what he was trying to describe was not only faith but love, and that it couldn't be done. Still smiling, he said, "You'll see, Porchoff. You'll get your chance."

Porchoff stared at Hooper. "You're crazy," he said.

"We're all going to get another chance," Hooper said. "I can feel it coming. Otherwise I'd take my walking papers and hat up. You'll see, Porchoff. All you need is a little contact. The rest of us too. Get us out of this rut."

Porchoff shook his head and murmured, "You're really crazy."

"Let's call it a day," Hooper said. He stood and held out his hand. "Give me the rifle."

"No," Porchoff said. He pulled the rifle closer. "Not to you."

"There's no one here but me," Hooper said.

"Go get Captain King."

"Captain King is asleep."

"Then wake him up."

"No," Hooper said. "I'm not going to tell you again, Porchoff, give me the rifle." Hooper walked toward him but stopped when Porchoff picked the weapon up and pointed it at his chest. "Leave me alone," Porchoff said.

"Relax," Hooper told him. "I'm not going to hurt you." He held out his hand again.

Porchoff licked his lips. "No," he said. "Not you."

Behind Hooper a voice called out, "Hey! Porkchop! Drop it!"

Porchoff sat bolt upright. "Jesus," he said.

"It's Trac," Hooper said. "Put the rifle down, Porchoff
— now!"

"Drop it!" Trac shouted.

"Oh Jesus," Porchoff said and stumbled to his feet with
the rifle still in his hands. Then his head flapped and his
helmet flew off and he toppled backwards over the bench.
Hooper's heart leaped as the shock of the blast hit him.
Then the sound went through him and beyond him and
into the trees and the sky, echoing on in the distance like
thunder. Afterwards there was silence. Hooper took a step
forward, then sank to his knees and lowered his forehead to
the wet grass. He spread his fingers through the grass
beside his head. The rain fell around him with a soft
whispering sound. A bluejay squawked. Another bird
called out, and then the trees grew loud with song.

Hooper heard the swish of boots through the grass
behind him. He pushed himself up and sat back on his
heels and drew a deep breath.

"You okay?" Trac said.

Hooper nodded.

Trac walked on to where Porchoff lay. He said something in Vietnamese, then looked back at Hooper and
shook his head.

Hooper tried to stand but went to his knees again.

"You need a hand?" Trac asked.

"I guess so," Hooper said.

Trac came over to Hooper. He slung his rifle and bent
down and the two men gripped each other's wrists. Trac's
skin was dry and smooth, his bones as small as a child's.
This close, he looked more familiar than ever. "Go for it,"
Trac said. He tensed as Hooper pulled himself to his feet
and for a moment afterwards they stood facing each other,
swaying slightly, hands still locked on one another's wrists.

"All right," Hooper said. Each of them slowly loosened his grip.

In a soft voice, almost a whisper, Trac said, "They gonna put me away?"

"No," Hooper said. He walked over to Porchoff and looked down at him. He immediately turned away and saw that Trac was still swaying, and that his eyes were glassy. "Better get off those legs," Hooper said. Trac looked at him dreamily, then unslung his rifle and leaned it against the picnic table farthest from Porchoff. He sat down and took his helmet off and rested his head on his crossed forearms.

The clouds had darkened. The wind was picking up again, carrying with it the whine of distant engines. Hooper fumbled a cigarette out of his case and smoked it down, staring toward the woods, feeling the rain stream down his face and neck. When the cigarette went out Hooper dropped it, then picked it up again and field-stripped it, crumbling the tobacco around his feet so that no trace of it remained. He put his cap back on and raised the hood of his poncho. "How's it going?" he said to Trac.

Trac looked up. He began to rub his forehead, pushing his fingers in little circles above his eyes.

Hooper sat down across from him. "We don't have a whole lot of time," he said.

Trac nodded. He put his helmet on and looked over at Hooper, the scar on his brow livid where he had rubbed it.

"All right, son," Hooper said. "Let's get our story together."

DESERT
BREAKDOWN, 1968

K rystal was asleep when they crossed the Colorado. Mark had promised to stop for some pictures, but when the moment came he looked over at her and drove on. Krystal's face was puffy from the heat blowing into the car. Her hair, cut short for summer, hung damp against her forehead. Only a few strands lifted in the breeze. She had her hands folded over her belly and that made her look even more pregnant than she was.

The tires sang on the metal grillwork of the bridge. The river stretched away on both sides, blue as the empty sky. Mark saw the shadow of the bridge on the water with the car running through the girders, and the glint of water under the grillwork. Then the tires went silent. *California*, Mark thought, and for a time he felt almost as good as he had expected to feel.

But it soon passed. He had broken his word, and he was going to hear about it when Krystal woke up. He almost turned the car around. But he didn't want to have to stop, and hoist Hans up on his shoulders, and watch Krystal point that camera at him again. By now Krystal had hundreds of pictures of Mark, Mark with Hans on his shoulders standing in front of canyons and waterfalls and monumental trees and the three automobiles they'd owned since coming Stateside.

Mark did not photograph well. For some reason he always looked discouraged. But those pictures gave the wrong idea. An old platoon sergeant of Mark's had an expression he liked to use — "free, white, and twenty-one." Well, that was an exact description of Mark. Everything was in front of him. All he needed was an opening.

Two hawks wheeled overhead, their shadows immense on the baking grey sand. A spinning funnel of dust moved across the road and disappeared behind a billboard. The billboard had a picture of Eugene McCarthy on it. Mc-Carthy's hair was blowing around his head. He was grinning. The caption below said, "A Breath of Fresh Air." You could tell this was California because in Arizona a McCarthy billboard would last about five minutes. This one had bullet holes in it, but in Arizona someone would have burned it down or blown it up. The people there were just incredibly backward.

In the distance the mountains were bare and blue. Mark passed exit signs for a town called Blythe. He considered stopping for some gas, but there was still half a tank and he did not want to risk waking Krystal or Hans. He drove on into the desert.

They would make Los Angeles by dinnertime. Mark had an army buddy there who'd offered to put them up for as long as they wanted to stay. There was plenty of room, his buddy had said. He was house-sitting for his parents while they made up their minds whether to get divorced or not.

Mark was sure he'd find something interesting in Los Angeles. Something in the entertainment field. He had been in plays all through high school and could sing pretty well. But his big talent was impersonation. He could mimic anybody. In Germany he had mimicked a Southern fellow in his company so accurately that after a couple of weeks of it the boy asked to be transferred to another unit. Mark knew he'd gone overboard. He laid off and in the end the boy withdrew his request for transfer.

His best impersonation was his father, Dutch. Sometimes, just for fun, Mark called his mother and talked to her in Dutch's slow, heavy voice, rolling every word along on treads, like a tank. She always fell for it. Mark would go on until he got bored, then say something like, "By the way, Dottie, we're bankrupt." Then she would catch on and laugh. Unlike Dutch, she had a sense of humor.

A truck hurtled past. The sound of the engine woke Hans, but Mark reached into the back and rubbed the satin edge of the baby blanket against Hans's cheek. Hans put his thumb in his mouth. Then he stuck his rear end in the air and went back to sleep.

The road shimmered. It seemed to float above the desert floor. Mark sang along with the radio, which he had been turning up as the signal grew weaker. Suddenly it blared. He turned it down, but he was too late. Hans woke up again and started fussing. Mark rubbed his cheek with the blanket. Hans pushed Mark's arm away and said, "No!" It was the only word he knew. Mark glanced back at him. He'd been sleeping on a toy car and the wheels had left four red dents on the side of his face. Mark stroked his cheek. "Pretty soon," he said, "pretty soon, Hansy," not meaning anything in particular but wanting to sound confident, upbeat.

Krystal was awake now too. For a moment she didn't move or say anything. Then she shook her head rapidly from side to side. "So hot," she said. She held up the locket-watch around her neck and looked at Mark. He kept his eyes on the road. "Back from the dead," he said. "Boy, you were really out."

"The pictures," she said. "Mark, the pictures."

"There wasn't any place to stop," he said.

"But you promised."

Mark looked at her, then back at the road. "I'm sorry," he said. "There'll be other rivers."

"I wanted that one," Krystal said, and turned away. Mark could tell that she was close to tears. It made him feel tired. "All right," he said. "Do you want me to go back?" He slowed the car to prove he meant it. "If that's what you want just say the word."

She shook her head.

Mark sped up.

Hans began to kick the back of the seat. Mark didn't say anything. At least it was keeping Hans busy and quiet. "Hey, gang," Mark said. "Listen up. I've got ten big ones that say we'll be diving into Rick's pool by six o'clock."

Hans gave the seat a kick that Mark felt clear through to his ribs. "Ten big ones," Mark said. "Any takers?" He looked over at Krystal and saw that her lips were trembling. He patted the seat beside him. She hesitated, then slid over and leaned against him, as he knew she would. Krystal was not one to hold a grudge. He put his arm around her shoulder.

"So much desert," she said.

"It's something, all right."

"No trees," she said. "At home I could never imagine."

Hans stopped kicking. Then, without warning, he grabbed Mark's ears. Krystal laughed and pulled him over the seat onto her lap. He immediately arched his back and slid down to the floor, where he began to tug at the gear shift.

"I have to stop," Krystal said. She patted her belly. "This one likes to sit just so, here, on my bladder."

Mark nodded. Krystal knew the English words for what Dottie had always been content to call her plumbing, and when she was pregnant she liked to describe in pretty close detail what went on in there. It made Mark queasy. "Next chance we get," he said. "We're low anyway."

Mark turned off at an exit with one sign that said GAS. There was no mention of a town.

The road went north over bleached hardpan crazed with fissures. It seemed to be leading them toward a solitary mountain far away that looked to Mark like a colossal sinking ship. Phantom water glistened in the desert. Rabbits darted back and forth across the road. Finally they came to the gas station, an unpainted cement-block building with some pickup trucks parked in front. Mark pulled in.

There were four men sitting on a bench in the shade of the building. They watched the car come toward them.

"Cowboys," Krystal said. "Look, Hans, cowboys!"

Hans stood on Krystal's legs and looked out the window.

Krystal still thought that everyone who wore a cowboy hat was a cowboy. Mark had tried to explain that it was a style, but she refused to understand. He drove up to a pump and turned off the engine.

The four men stared at them. Their faces were dark under the wide brims of their hats. They looked as if they had been there forever. One of the men got up from the bench and walked over. He was tall and carried a paunch that seemed out of place on his bony frame. He bent down and looked inside the car. He had little black eyes with no eyebrows. His face was red, as if he were angry about something.

"Regular, please," Mark said. "All she'll take."

The man stared openly at Krystal's belly. He straightened up and walked away, past the men on the bench, up to the open door of the building. He stuck his head inside and yelled. Then he sat on the bench again. The man next to him looked down and mumbled something. The others laughed.

Somebody else in a cowboy hat came out of the building and went around to the back of the car. "Mark," Krystal said.

"I know," Mark said. "The bathroom." He got out of the car. The heat took him by surprise; he could feel it coming down like rain. The person pumping gas said, "You need oil or anything?" and that was when Mark realized it was a woman. She was looking down at the nozzle, so he couldn't see her face, only the top of her hat. Her hands were black with grease. "My wife would like to use your bathroom," he said.

She nodded. When the tank was full she thumped on the roof of the car. "Okay," she said, and walked toward the building.

Krystal opened the door. She swung her legs out, then rocked forward and pushed herself up into the light. She stood for a moment, blinking. The four men looked at her. So did Mark. He made allowances for the fact that Krystal was pregnant, but she was still too heavy. Her bare arms were flushed from the heat. So was her face. She looked like one of those stein-slinging waitresses in the *Biergarten* where she and Mark used to drink. He wished that these fellows could have seen the way Krystal looked wearing that black dress of hers, with her hair long, when they'd first started going out together.

Krystal shaded her eyes with one hand. With the other hand she pulled her blouse away from where it stuck to her skin. "More desert," she said. She lifted Hans out of the car and began to carry him toward the building, but he kicked free and ran over to the bench. He stood there in front of the men, naked except for his diaper.

"Come here," Krystal said. When he didn't obey she started toward him, then looked at the men and stopped. Mark went over. "Let's go, Hansy," he said. He picked Hans up, and felt a sudden tenderness that vanished when Hans began to struggle.

The woman took Krystal and Hans inside the building, then came out and sat on the pile of scrap lumber beside the door. "Hans," she said. "That's a funny name for a little boy."

"It was her father's name," Mark said, and so it was. The original Hans had died shortly before the baby was born. Otherwise Mark never would have agreed. Even Germans didn't name their kids Hans anymore.

One of the men flicked a cigarette butt toward Mark's car. It fell just short and lay there, smoldering. Mark took it as a judgment on the car. It was a good car, a 1958 Bonneville he'd bought two weeks ago when the Ford started to smoke, but a previous owner had put a lot of extra chrome on it and right now it was gleaming every which way. It looked foolish next to these dented pickups with their gun racks and dull blistering paint. Mark wished he'd tanked up in Blythe.

Krystal came outside again, carrying Hans. She had brushed her hair and looked better.

Mark smiled at her. "All set?"

She nodded. "Thank you," she said to the woman.

Mark would have liked to use the bathroom too, but he wanted to get out of there. He started toward the car, Krystal behind him. She laughed deep in her throat. "You should have seen," she said. "They have a motorcycle in their bedroom." Krystal probably thought she was whispering but to Mark every word was like a shout.

He didn't say anything. He adjusted the visor while Krystal settled Hans on the back seat. "Wait," she told Mark, and got out of the car again. She had the camera.

"Krystal," Mark said.

She aimed the camera at the four men. When she snapped the shutter their heads jerked up. Krystal advanced the film, then aimed the camera again.

Mark said, "Krystal, get in!"

"Yes," Krystal said, but she was still aiming, braced on the open door of the car, her knees bent slightly. She snapped another picture and slid onto the seat. "Good," she said. "Cowboys for Reiner."

Reiner was Krystal's brother. He had seen *Shane* more than a hundred times.

Mark didn't dare look toward the bench. He put the key in the ignition and glanced up and down the road. He turned the key. Nothing happened.

Mark took a deep breath and waited for a moment. Then he tried again. Still nothing happened. The ignition went *tick tick tick tick*, and that was all. Mark turned it off and the three of them sat there. Even Hans was quiet. Mark felt the men watching him. That was why he did not lower his head to the wheel and give way to tears. But they were in his eyes, blurring the line of the horizon, the shape of the building, the dark forms of the trucks and the figure coming toward them over the white earth.

It was the woman. She bent down. "Okay," she said. "What's the trouble?" The smell of whiskey filled the car.

For almost half an hour the woman messed with the engine. She had Mark turn the key while she watched, then turn it some more while she did various things under the hood. At last she decided that the trouble was in the alternator. She couldn't fix it, and she had no parts on hand. Mark would have to get one in Indio or Blythe or maybe as far away as Palm Springs. It wasn't going to be easy, finding an alternator for a ten-year-old car. But she said she'd call around for him.

Mark waited in the car. He tried to act as if everything were all right, but when Krystal looked at him she made a sympathetic noise and squeezed his arm. Hans was asleep in her lap. "Everything will be fine," Krystal said.

Mark nodded.

The woman came back toward the car, and Mark got out to meet her.

"Aren't you the lucky one," she said. She gave Mark a piece of paper with an address written on it. "There wasn't anything in Indio," she said, "but this fellow in Blythe can fix you up. I'll need two dollars for the calls."

Mark opened his wallet and gave her the two dollars. He had sixty-five dollars left, all that remained of his army severance pay. "How much will the alternator cost?" he asked.

She closed the hood of the car. "Fifty-eight ninety-nine, I think it was."

"Jesus," Mark said.

The woman shrugged. "You're lucky they had one."

"I suppose so," Mark said. "It just seems like a lot of money. Can you jump-start me?"

"If you've got cables. Mine are lent out."

"I don't have any," Mark said. He squinted against the sun. Though he had not looked directly at the men on the bench, he knew that they had been watching him. He was sure that they had heard everything. He was also sure that they had jumper cables. People who drove trucks always carried stuff like that.

But if they didn't want to help, he wasn't going to ask.

"I guess I could walk up to the highway and hitch a ride," Mark said, more loudly than he meant to.

"I guess you could," the woman said.

Mark looked back at Krystal. "Is it okay if my wife stays here?"

"I guess she'll have to," the woman said. She took off her hat and wiped her brow with the back of her sleeve. Her hair was pure yellow, gathered in a loose bun that glowed in the light. Her eyes were black. She put her hat back on and told Mark how to get to the parts store. She made him repeat the directions. Then he went back to the car.

Krystal looked straight ahead and bit her lip while Mark explained the situation. "Here?" she said. "You are going to leave us here?"

Hans was awake again. He had pulled the volume knob off the radio and was banging it on the dashboard.

"Just for a couple of hours," Mark said, though he knew it would take twice as long, maybe longer.

Krystal wouldn't look at him.

"There's no choice," he said.

The woman had been standing next to Mark. She moved

him aside and opened the door. "You come with me," she said. "You and the little one." She held out her arms. Hans went to her immediately and peered over her shoulder at the men on the bench. Krystal hesitated, then got out of the car, ignoring Mark's hand when he reached down to help her.

"It won't take long," he said. He smiled at Hans. "Pretty soon, Hansy," he said, and turned and began to walk toward the road.

The woman went inside with Hans. Krystal stood beside the car and watched Mark move farther and farther away, until the line of his body started to waver in the heat and then vanished altogether. This happened suddenly. It was like seeing someone slip below the surface of a lake.

The men stared at Krystal as she walked toward the building. She felt heavy, and vaguely ashamed.

The woman had all the shades pulled down. It was like evening inside: dim, peaceful, cool. Krystal could make out the shapes of things but not their colors. There were two rooms. One had a bed and a motorcycle. The second, big room had a sofa and chairs on one side and on the other a refrigerator and stove and table.

Krystal sat at the table with Hans in her lap while the woman poured Pepsi from a big bottle into three tumblers full of ice. She had taken her hat off, and the weak light shining from the open door of the refrigerator made a halo around her face and hair. Usually Krystal measured herself against other women, but this one she watched with innocent, almost animal curiosity.

The woman took another, smaller bottle down from the top of the refrigerator. She wiggled it by the neck. "You wouldn't want any of this," she said. Krystal shook her head. The woman poured some of the liquor into her glass and pushed the other two glasses across the table. Hans took a drink, then began to make motorboat noises.

"That boy," the woman said.

"His name is Hans."

"Not this one," the woman said. "The other one."

"Oh," Krystal said. "Mark. Mark is my husband."

The woman nodded and took a drink. She leaned back in her chair. "Where are you people headed?"

Krystal told her about Los Angeles, about Mark finding work in the entertainment field. The woman smiled, and Krystal wondered if she had expressed herself correctly. In school she had done well in English, and the American boys she talked to always complimented her, but during those weeks with Mark's parents in Phoenix she had lost her confidence. Dutch and Dottie always looked bewildered when she spoke, and she herself understood almost nothing of what was said around her though she pretended that she did.

The woman kept smiling, but there was a tightness to her mouth that made the smile look painful somehow. She took another drink. "What does he do?" she asked.

Krystal tried to think of a way to explain what Mark did. When she first saw him, he had been sitting on the floor at a party and everyone around him was laughing. She had laughed too, though she didn't know why. It was a gift he had. But it was difficult to put into words. "Mark is a singer," she said.

"A singer," the woman said. She closed her eyes and leaned her head back and began to sing. Hans stopped fidgeting and watched her.

When the woman was through, Krystal said, "Good, good," and nodded, though she hadn't been able to follow the song and hated the style, which sounded to her like yodeling.

"My husband always liked to hear me sing," the woman said. "I suppose I could have been a singer if I'd wanted." She finished her drink and looked at the empty glass.

From outside Krystal heard the voices of the men on the bench, low and steady. One of them laughed.

"We had Del Ray to sing at our prom," the woman said.

The door banged. The man who'd stared at Krystal's belly stomped into the kitchen and stared at her again. The woman smiled at him. The tightness left her mouth and her lips parted slightly, as if she were about to say something. He turned and started pulling bottles of Pepsi out of the refrigerator. "Webb, what do you think?" the woman said. "This girl's husband's a singer." She reached out and ran one hand up and down his back. "We'll need something for supper," she said, "unless you want rabbit again."

He kicked the refrigerator door shut with his foot and started out of the kitchen, bottles clinking against each other. Hans slid to the floor and ran after him.

"Hans," Krystal said.

The man stopped and looked down at him. "That's right," he said. "You come with me."

It was the first time Krystal had heard him speak. His voice was thin and dry. He went back outside with Hans behind him.

The shoes Mark had on were old and loose, comfortable in the car, but his feet started to burn after a few minutes

of walking in them. His eyes burned too, from sweat and
the bright sun shining into his face.

For a while he sang songs, but after a couple of numbers
his throat cracked with dryness so he gave it up. Anyway
it made him feel stupid singing about Camelot in this
desert, stupid and a little afraid because his voice sounded
so small. He walked on.

The road was sticky underfoot. Mark's shoes made little
sucking noises at every step. He considered walking beside
the road instead of on it but he was afraid that a snake
would bite him.

He wanted to stay cheerful, but he kept thinking that
now they would never get to Los Angeles in time for
dinner. They'd pull in late like they always did, stuff
spilling out of the car, Mark humping the whole mess
inside while Krystal stood by looking dazed in the glare
of the headlights, Hans draped over her shoulder. Mark's
buddy would be in his bathrobe. They'd try to joke but
Mark would be too preoccupied. After they made up a
bed for Krystal and put the crib together for Hans, which
would take forever because half the screws were missing,
Mark and his buddy would go down to the kitchen and
drink a beer. They'd try to talk but they would end up
yawning in each other's faces. Then they would go to bed.

Mark could see the whole thing. Whatever they did, it
always turned out like this. Nothing ever worked.

A truck went past going the other way. There were two
men inside wearing cowboy hats. They glanced at Mark,
then looked straight ahead again. He stopped and watched
the truck disappear into the heat.

He turned and kept walking. Broken glass glittered
along the roadside.

If Mark lived here and happened to be driving down

this road and saw some person walking all by himself, he
would stop and ask if there was anything wrong. He believed in helping people.

But he didn't need them. He would manage without
them, just as he'd manage without Dutch and Dottie. He
would do it alone, and someday they would wish they'd
helped. He would be in some place like Las Vegas, per-
forming at one of the big clubs. Then, at the end of his
booking, he would fly Dutch and Dottie out for his last
big show — the finale. He'd fly them first class and put
them up in the best hotel, the Sands or whatever, and he'd
get them front row seats. And when the show was over,
when the people were going crazy, whistling and stamping
on the floor and everything, he would call Dutch and
Dottie up to the stage. He would stand between them,
holding their hands, and then, when all the clapping and
yelling trailed off and everybody was quiet, smiling at him
from the tables, he would raise Dutch and Dottie's hands
above his head and say, Folks, I just wanted you to meet
my parents and tell you what they did for me. He would
stop for a second and get this really serious look on his
face. It's impossible to tell you what they did for me, he
would say, pausing for effect — because they didn't do
anything for me! They didn't do *squat* for me!

Then he would drop their hands and jump off the stage
and leave them there.

Mark walked faster, leaning forward, eyes narrowed
against the light. His hands flicked back and forth as he
walked.

No, he wouldn't do that. People might take it wrong.
A stunt like that could ruin his career. He would do something even better. He would stand up there and tell the
whole world that without the encouragement and support

the two of them had given him, the faith and love, et cetera, he would have thrown in the towel a long time ago.

And the great part was, *it wouldn't be true!* Because Dutch and Dottie wouldn't do a thing for him unless he stayed in Phoenix and got a "real job" — like selling houses. But nobody would know that except Dutch and Dottie. They would stand up on the stage listening to all those lies, and the more he complimented them the more they would see the kind of parents they could have been and weren't, and the more ashamed they would feel, and the more grateful to Mark for not exposing them.

He could hear a faint rushing sound in the hot air, a sound like applause. He walked faster still. He hardly felt the burning of his feet. The rushing sound grew louder, and Mark looked up. Ahead of him, no more than a hundred yards off, he saw the highway — not the road itself, but a long convoy of trucks moving across the desert, floating westward through a blue haze of exhaust.

The woman told Krystal that her name was Hope.

"Hope," Krystal said. "How lovely."

They were in the bedroom. Hope was working on the motorcycle. Krystal lay on the bed, propped up with pillows, watching Hope's long fingers move here and there over the machine and through the parts on the floor, back to the sweating glass at her side. Hans was outside with the men.

Hope took a drink. She swirled the ice around and said, "I don't know, Krystal."

Krystal felt the baby move in her. She folded her hands across her belly and waited for the bump to come again.

All the lights were off except for a lamp on the floor

beside Hope. There were engine parts scattered around her, and the air smelled of oil. She picked up a part and looked at it, then began to wipe it down with a cloth. "I told you we had Del Ray to our prom," she said. "I don't know if you ever heard of Del Ray where you came from, but us girls were flat crazy about him. I had a Del Ray pillow I slept on. Then he showed up and it turned out he was only about yay high." Hope held her hand a few inches above the floor. "Personally," she said, "I wouldn't look twice at a man that couldn't stand up for me if it came to the point. No offense," she added.

Krystal didn't understand what Hope had said, so she smiled.

"You take Webb," Hope said. "Webb would kill for me. He almost did, once. He beat a man to an inch of his life."

Krystal understood this. She felt sure it was true. She ran her tongue over her dry lips. "Who?" she asked. "Who did he beat?"

Hope looked up from the part she was cleaning. She smiled at Krystal in such a way that Krystal had to smile back.

"My husband," Hope said. She looked down again, still smiling.

Krystal waited, uncertain whether she had heard Hope right.

"Webb and me were hot," Hope said. "We were an item. When we weren't together, which was most of the time, we were checking up on each other. Webb used to drive past my house at all hours and follow me everywhere. Sometimes he'd follow me places with his wife in the car next to him." She laughed. "It was a situation."

The baby was pressing against Krystal's spine. She shifted slightly.

Hope looked up at her. "It's a long story."

"Tell me."

"I need some mouthwash," Hope said. She got up and went out to the kitchen. Krystal heard the crack of an ice tray. It was pleasant to lie here in this dark, cool room.

Hope came back and settled on the floor. "Don't get me going," she said. She took a drink. "The long and the short is, Webb lost his senses. It happened at the movie theater in front of half the town. Webb was sitting behind us and saw my husband put his arm around me. He came right over the chairs." She shook her head. "I can tell you we did some fancy footwork after that. Had to. My husband had six brothers and two of them in the police. We got out of there and I mean we *got*. Nothing but the clothes we had on. Never gone back since. Never will, either."

"Never," Krystal said. She admired the sound of the word. It was like Beethoven shaking his fist at the heavens.

Hope picked up the rag again. But she didn't do anything with it. She leaned against the wall, out of the little circle of light the lamp made.

"Did you have children?" Krystal asked.

Hope nodded. She held up two fingers.

"It must be hard, not to see them."

"Sometimes. Not all that much. The thing about kids, they don't leave you any room. They crowd you out of your own life. You know what I mean."

Krystal nodded.

"They'll do all right," Hope said. "They're both boys." She ran her fingers over the floor, found the part she'd been cleaning, and without looking at it began to wipe it down again.

"I couldn't leave Hans," Krystal said.

"Sure you could," Hope said. The motion of her arms slowed. She grew still. "I remember when I fell for Webb. We'd known him for years, but this one day he came into our station on his Harley. It was cold. His cheeks were red and his hair was all blown back. I remember it like it was yesterday."

Hope sat there with her hands in her lap. Her breathing got deep and slow, and Krystal, peering through the gloom, saw that her eyes were closed. She was asleep, or just dreaming — maybe of that man out there riding over the desert on this machine, his hair pushed back in the way that was special to her.

Krystal settled herself on her side. The baby was quiet now.

The air conditioner went off abruptly. Krystal lay in the dark and listened to the sounds it had covered, the dry whirr of insects, the low voices of the men, Hope's soft snoring. Krystal closed her eyes. She felt herself drifting, and as she drifted she remembered Hans. *Hans,* she thought. Then she slept.

Mark had assumed that when he reached the highway someone would immediately pick him up. But car after car went by, and the few drivers who looked at him scowled as if they were angry with him for needing a ride and putting them on the spot.

Mark's face burned, and his throat was so dry it hurt to swallow. Twice he had to leave the road to stand in the shade of a billboard. Cars passed him by for more than an hour, cars from Wisconsin and Utah and Georgia and just about everywhere. Mark felt like the whole country had turned its back on him. The thought came to him that he could die out here.

Finally a car stopped. It was a hearse. Mark hesitated, then ran toward it.

There were three people in the front seat, a man between two women. There was no rear seat. The space in back was full of electrical equipment. Mark pushed some wires out of his way and sat cross-legged on the floor. He felt the breeze from the air conditioner; it was like a stream of cold water running over him.

The driver pulled back onto the road.

"Welcome to the stiffmobile," said the man beside her. He turned around. His head was shaved except for one bristling stripe of hair down the center. It was the first Mohawk haircut Mark had ever seen. The man's eyebrows were the same carroty color as his hair. He had freckles. The freckles covered his entire face and even the shaved parts of his skull.

"Stiffmobile, cliffmobile," said the woman driving. "Riffmobile."

"Bet you thought you'd be riding with a cold one," the man said.

Mark shrugged. "I'd rather ride with a cold one than a hot one."

The man laughed and pounded on the back of the seat. The two women also laughed. The one not driving turned around and smiled at Mark. She had a round, soft-looking face. Her lips were full. She wore a small gold earring in one side of her nose. "Hi," she said.

"Speaking of cold ones," the man said, "there's a case of them right behind you."

Mark fished four cans of beer out of the cooler and passed three of them up front. He took a long swallow, head back, eyes closed. When he opened his eyes again the man with the Mohawk was watching him. They introduced themselves, all but the woman driving. She never looked at Mark or spoke, except to herself. The man with the Mohawk was Barney. The girl with the earring was Nance. They joked back and forth, and Mark discovered that Nance had a terrific sense of humor. She picked up on almost everything he said. After a while the earring in her nose ceased to bother him.

When Barney heard that Mark had been in the army he shook his head. "Pass on that," he said. "No bang-bang for Barney. I can't stand the sight of my own brains."

"Trains," the driver said. "Cranes, lanes, stains."

"Smoothe out," Barney told her. He turned back to Mark. "So what was it like over there?"

Mark realized that Barney meant Vietnam. Mark had not been to Vietnam. He'd had orders to go, but the orders were killed just before he left and never reissued. He didn't know why. It was too complicated to explain, so he just said, "Pretty bad," and left it at that.

"Wrong question," Barney said. "That subject is strictly underwater. Scout's honor." He held up three fingers.

The mention of Vietnam broke the good feeling between them. They drank their beers and looked at the desert passing by. Then Barney crumpled his can and threw it out the window. Hot air blew into Mark's face. He remembered what it was like out there, and felt glad to be right where he was.

"I could get behind another beer," Nance said.

"Right," Barney said. He turned around and told Mark

to pop some more frosties. While Mark was getting the cans out of the cooler Barney watched him, playing his fingers over the top of the seat as if it were a keyboard. "So what's in Blythe?" he said.

"Smythe," the driver said. "Smythe's in Blythe."

"Be cool," Nance said to her.

"I need a part," Mark said. He handed out the beers. "An alternator. My car's on the fritz."

"Where's your car?" Barney said.

Mark jerked his thumb over his shoulder. "Back there. I don't know the name of the place. It's just this gas station off the highway." Nance was looking at him. He smiled. She kept watching him.

"Hey," she said. "What if you didn't stop smiling? What if you just kept smiling and never stopped?"

Barney looked at her. Then he looked back at Mark. "To me," he said, "there are places you go and places you don't go. You don't go to Rochester. You don't go to Blythe."

"You definitely don't go to Blythe," Nance said.

"Right," Barney said. Then he listed some of the places where, in his opinion, you do go. They were going to one of them now, San Lucas, up in the mountains above Santa Fe. They were part of a film crew shooting a Western there. They had shot another movie in the same place a year ago and this was the sequel. Barney was a sound man. Nance did make-up. They didn't say anything about the driver.

"The place is unbelievable," Barney said. He paused and shook his head. Mark was waiting for him to describe San Lucas, but Barney just shook his head again and said, "The place is completely unbelievable."

"Really," Nance said.

It turned out that the star of the picture was Nita Damon. This was a real coincidence, because Mark had seen Nita Damon about six months ago in a show in Germany, a Bob Hope Christmas Special.

"That's amazing," Nance said. She and Barney looked at each other. "You should scratch Blythe," Barney said. Mark grinned.

Nance was staring at him. "Marco," she said. "You're not a Mark, you're a Marco."

"You should sign on with us," Barney said. "Ride the stiffmobile express."

"You should," Nance said. "San Lucas is just incredible."

"Partyville," Barney said.

"Jesus," Mark said. "No. I couldn't."

"Sure you could," Barney said. "Lincoln freed the slaves, didn't he? Get your car later."

Mark was laughing. "Come on," he said. "What would I do up there?"

Barney said, "You mean like work?"

Mark nodded.

"No problem," Barney said. He told Mark that there was always something to do. People didn't show up, people quit, people got sick — there was always a call out for warm bodies. Once you found a tasty spot, you just settled in.

"You mean I'd be working on the movie? On the film crew?"

"Absitively," Barney said. "I guarantee."

"Jesus," Mark said. He took a breath. He looked at Barney and Nance. "I don't know," he said.

"That's all right," Barney said. "I know."

"Barney knows," Nance said.

"What have you got to lose?" Barney said.

Mark didn't say anything. He took another breath.

Barney watched him. "Marco," he said. "Don't tell me — you've got a little something else back there besides the car, right?" When Mark didn't answer, Barney laughed. "That's mellow," he said. "You're among friends. Anything goes."

"I have to think," Mark said.

"Okay," Barney said. "Think. You've got till Blythe." He turned around. "Don't disappoint me," he said.

Nance smiled. Then she turned around too. The top of her head was just visible over the high seat-back.

The desert went past the window, always the same. The road had an oily look. Mark felt rushed, a little wild.

His first idea was to get the directions to San Lucas, then drive up with Krystal and Hans after the car was fixed. But that wouldn't work. He wouldn't have enough money left for the gas, let alone food and motels and a place to live once they got there. He'd miss his chance.

Because that's what this was — a chance.

There was no point in fooling himself. He could go to Los Angeles and walk the streets for months, years maybe, without ever getting anywhere. He could stand outside closed doors and suck up to nobodies and sit in plastic chairs half his life without ever coming close to where he was right now, on his way to a guaranteed job in Partyville.

Los Angeles wasn't going to work. Mark could see that. He'd borrow money from his friend and start hustling and he wouldn't get the time of day from anyone, because he was hungry, and nobody ever had time for hungry people. Hungry people got written off. It was like Dutch said — them as has, gets.

He would run himself ragged and the money would disappear, the way all his other money had disappeared. Krystal would get worried and sad. After a couple of weeks Mark and his buddy wouldn't have anything to say to each other, and his buddy would get tired of living with a guy he didn't really know that well and a yelling kid and a sad, pregnant woman. He would tell Mark some lie to get rid of them — his girl was moving in, his parents had decided to stay together after all. By then Mark would be broke again. Krystal would have a fit and probably go into labor.

What if that happened? What then?

Mark knew what. Crawl home to Dutch and Dottie.

No. No sir. The only way he was going back to Phoenix was in a coffin.

The driver started talking to herself. Barney rapped her on top of the head with his knuckles. "Do you want me to drive?" he said. It sounded like a threat. She quieted down. "All right," he said. Without looking back he said, "Five miles to Blythe."

Mark looked out the window. He couldn't get it out of his mind that here he had exactly what he needed. A chance to show what he was made of. He'd have fun, sure, but he'd also be at work on time in the morning. He would do what he was told and do it right. He would keep his eyes open and his mouth shut and after a while people would start to notice him. He wouldn't push too hard, but now and then he might do a song at one of the parties, or impersonate some of the actors. He could just hear Nita Damon laughing and saying, "Stop it, Mark! Stop it!"

What he could do, Mark thought, was to call Krystal and arrange to meet up with her at his buddy's house in a month or two, after they'd shot the film. Mark would have something going then. He'd be on his way. But that wouldn't work, either. He didn't know how to call her. She had no money. And she wouldn't agree.

Mark wasn't going to fool himself. If he left Krystal and Hans back there, she would never forgive him. If he left them, he left them for good.

I can't do that, Mark thought. But he knew this wasn't true. He had decided not to fool himself, and that meant being honest about everything. He could leave them. People left one another, and got left, every day. It was a terrible thing. But it happened and people survived, as they survived worse things. Krystal and Hans would survive, too. When she understood what had happened she would call Dutch. Dutch would hit the roof, but in the end he would come through for them. He didn't have any choice. And in four or five years what happened today would be nothing but a bad memory.

Krystal would do well for herself. Men liked her. Even Dutch liked her, though he'd been dead set against the marriage. She would meet a good man someday, a man who could take care of her. She and Hans and the new baby would be able to go to sleep at night without wondering what would happen to them when they woke up. They didn't need Mark. Without him they would have a better life than if he and Krystal stayed together.

This was a new thought for Mark, and when he had it he felt aggrieved. It hurt him to see how unimportant he really was to Krystal. Before now he had always assumed that their coming together had somehow been ordained, and that in marrying Krystal he had filled some need of the universe. But if they could live without each other, and do better without each other, then this could not be true and must never have been true.

They did not need each other. There was no particular reason for them to be together. Then what was it all about? If he couldn't make her happy, then what was the point? They were dragging each other down like two people who couldn't swim. If they were lucky, they might keep at it long enough to grow old in the same house.

That was what they had to look forward to if they were lucky.

It wasn't right. She deserved better, and so did he.

Mark felt that he had been deceived, played with. Not by Krystal, she would never do that, but by everyone who had ever been married and knew the truth about it and went on acting as if it were something good. The truth was different. The truth was that when you got married you had to give up one thing after another. It never ended. You had to give up your life — the special one that you were meant to have — and lead some middle kind of life that went where neither of you had ever thought of going, or wanted to go. And you never knew what was happening. You gave up your life and didn't even know it.

"Blythe," Barney said.

Mark looked at the town, what he could see of it from the road. Lines of heat quivered above the rooftops.

"Blythe," Barney said again. "Going, going, gone."

When Krystal came up from sleep she expected to open her eyes on the sight of water, the great Colorado River. She had been dreaming that she was in the car with Mark and Hans, that it was still morning and this day had not happened yet. She blinked in the gloom. In a moment she knew where she was.

"Hans," she whispered.

"He's outside," Hope said. Hope was standing over the lamp, feeding shells into a shotgun. Her shadow swayed back and forth against the wall. "I'm going to get us some dinner," she said. "You just lie here and rest up. The boy will be fine." She finished loading the gun and pushed a few more shells into the pockets of her jeans. "Be right back," she said.

Krystal lay on the bed, restless and thirsty, but feeling too heavy to rise. Outside the men had a radio on. One of those whiny songs was playing, like Hope had sung in the kitchen. Krystal had heard no good music for two months now, since the day she left home. A warm day in late spring — lieder playing on the radio, sunlight flickering through the trees along the road. On the bridge leading out of town her mother had stopped the car to watch a swan paddling upstream with two cygnets behind her.

"Ah, God," Krystal said.

She pushed herself up. She lifted the shade of the window and looked out. There was the desert, and the mountains. And there was Hope, walking into the desert with her shotgun. The light was softer than before, still white but not so sharp. The tops of the mountains were touched with pink.

Krystal stared out the window. How could anyone live in such a place? There was nothing, nothing at all. Through all those days in Phoenix, Krystal had felt a great emptiness around her where she would count for no more than a rock or a spiny tree; now she was there.

Krystal thought she might cry, but she gave the idea up. It didn't interest her.

She closed her eyes and leaned her forehead against the glass.

I will say a poem, Krystal thought, and when I am finished he will be here. At first silently, because she had promised to speak only English now, then in a whisper, and at last plainly, Krystal recited a poem the nuns had made her learn at school long ago, the only poem she remembered. She repeated it twice, then opened her eyes. Mark was not there. As if she had really believed he would be there, Krystal kicked the wall with her bare foot. The pain gave an edge of absolute clarity to what she'd been pretending not to know: that of course he wouldn't be there, because he had never really been there and was never going to be there in any way that mattered.

The window was hot under Krystal's forehead. She watched Hope move farther and farther away. Then Hope stopped. She raised her gun. A moment later Krystal heard the boom, and felt the glass shudder against her skin.

A few miles past Blythe the driver began to talk to herself again. Her voice was flat. Mark looked out the window and tried to ignore it but after a time he found himself listening, trying to make sense of the things she said. There wasn't any reason to her words. Every possibility of meaning ended in the beginning of another possibility. It was frustrating to Mark. He became uncomfortable.

Then he noticed that the hearse was moving at great speed, really racing. The driver passed every car they came upon. She changed lanes without any purpose.

Mark tried to find a break between her words to say something, just a note of caution, something about how tough the police were around here, but no break came. The car was going faster and faster. He hoped that Barney would tell her to shut up and slow down, maybe even take over himself for a while, but Barney wasn't saying anything and neither was Nance. She had disappeared completely and all Mark could see of Barney were the bristles of his hair.

"Hey," Mark said. "What's the hurry?"

The driver seemed not to hear him. She passed three more cars and went on talking to herself. Then Mark saw that she had only one hand on the steering wheel, her left hand. She was gripping the wheel so tightly that her hand had turned white. He could see the bones of her fingers.

"Better slow down," Mark said.

"Blue horse sells kisses," she said, then repeated the words.

"Jesus," Mark said. He bent forward and leaned over the top of the seat to get a look at the speedometer. Then he saw what was going on up there and sat back. He had never seen anything like that before. It took the wind out of him. He felt far, far away from himself. Then the hearse started to shimmy. The driver was making what sounded like animal noises in the jungle. Nance giggled.

"Stop the car," Mark said.

"Stop the war," the driver said.

"Stop the car," Mark said again.

"Hey," Barney said. "What's the problem?" His voice was soft, remote.

"I want out," Mark said.

Nance giggled again. The tires began to whine.

"Everything's sweet," Barney said. "Just settle into it, Marco. You decided, remember?"

Mark didn't know what to say. It was hard to talk to someone he couldn't see.

He heard Nance whispering. Then Barney said, "Hey — Marco. Come on up here."

"Midnight phone book," the driver said.

"Come on," Barney said. "You're with us now."

"Stop the car," Mark said. He reached over the seat and began to rap on the driver's head, softly at first, then hard. He could hear the knocking of his knuckles against her skull. She turned and smiled at him. Her face was white. That was all he saw, the whiteness of her face, before she turned again. She stopped the hearse in the middle of the road. Mark looked back. There was a car bearing down on them. It swerved into the other lane and went past with its horn wailing.

"Okay, Marco," Barney said. "Ciao. You blew it."

Mark scrambled over equipment and cords and let himself out the back. When he closed the gate the driver pulled away, fast. Mark crossed the road and watched the hearse until it disappeared. The road was empty. He turned and walked back toward Blythe.

A few minutes later an old man stopped for him. He took a liking to Mark and drove him all the way to the parts store. They were closing up when he arrived, but after Mark explained his situation the boss let him inside and found the alternator for him. With tax, the price came to seventy-one dollars.

"I thought it was fifty-eight," Mark said.

"Seventy-one," the boss said.

Mark showed him the figures that the woman had written down, but it did no good. "Jesus," Mark said. He stared at the alternator. "I've only got sixty-five."

"I'm sorry," the boss said. He put his hands on the counter and waited.

"Look," Mark said. "I just got back from Vietnam. Me and my wife are on our way to Los Angeles. Once we get there I can send you the other six. I'll put it in the mail tomorrow morning. I swear."

The boss looked at him. Mark could see that he was hesitating.

"I've got a job waiting," Mark said.

"What kind of job?"

"I'm a sound man," Mark said.

"Sound man." The boss nodded. "I'm sorry," he said. "You think you'll send the money but you won't."

Mark argued for a while but without heat, because he knew that the man was right — he would never send the money. He gave up and went outside again. The parts store adjoined a salvage yard filled with crumpled cars. Across the street there was a U-Haul depot and a gas station. Mark began to walk toward the gas station. A black dog appeared on the other side of the salvage yard fence and kept pace with Mark. When Mark looked at him, the dog silently bared his fangs and gave Mark such a fright that he crossed the street.

He was hot and tired. He could smell himself. He remembered the coolness of the hearse and thought, *I blew it.*

There was a pay phone outside the gas station. Mark got a handful of change and shut himself in. He wanted to call his buddy in Los Angeles and figure something out, but he had left the address book in the car and it turned out that the number was unlisted. He tried to explain things to the operator but she refused to listen. She hung up on him.

Mark looked out at the street. The dog was still at the

fence, watching him. The only thing he could do, Mark decided, was to keep calling Los Angeles information until he got a human being on the other end. There had to be somebody sympathetic out there.

But first he was going to call Phoenix and give Dutch and Dottie a little something to sleep on. He would put on his official voice and tell them that he was Sergeant Smith — no, *Smythe* — Sergeant Smythe of the highway patrol, calling to report an accident. A head-on collision just outside of Palm Springs. It was his duty, he was sorry to say — his voice would crack — there were no survivors. No, ma'am, not one. Yes, ma'am, he was sure. He'd been at the scene. The one good thing he could tell her was that nobody had suffered. It was over just like *that*, and here Mark would snap his fingers into the receiver.

He closed his eyes and listened to the phone ring through the cool, quiet house. He saw Dottie where she sat in her avocado kitchen, drinking coffee and making a list, saw her rise and gather her cigarettes and lighter and ashtray. He heard her shoes tapping on the tile floor as she came toward the phone.

But it was Dutch who answered. "Strick here," he said.

Mark took a breath.

"Hello," Dutch said.

"It's me," Mark said. "Dad, it's me — Mark."

Krystal was washing her face when she heard the gun go off again. She paused, water running through her fingers, then finished up and left the bedroom. She wanted to find Hans. He should have been changed long before now, and it was almost time for him to eat. She missed him.

Picking her way through the parts on the floor, she went

into the main room. It was almost completely dark. Krystal felt her way along the wall to the light switch. She turned the light on and stood there with her hand against the wall.

Everything was red. The carpet was red. The lamp-shades were red, and had little red tassels hanging down from them. The chairs and the couch were red. The pillows on the couch were shaped like hearts and covered in a satiny material that looked wet under the light, so that for a moment they had the appearance of real organs.

Krystal stared at the room. In a novel she'd once read she had come upon the expression "love nest," and after considering it for a moment imagined light-washed walls, tall pines reaching to the balcony outside, an old bed with spiraling posts and a hunting scene carved across the head-board. But this, she thought, looking at the room, this was a love nest. It was horrible, horrible.

Krystal moved over to the door and opened it a crack. Someone was lying on the front seat of the car, his bare feet sticking out the window, his boots on the ground below with yellow socks hanging from the tops. She could not see the men on the bench but one of them was saying something, the same word again and again. Krystal couldn't make it out. Then she heard Hans repeat the word, and the men laughed.

She opened the door wider. Still standing inside, she said, "Hans, come here."

She waited. She heard someone whisper.

"Hans," she said.

He came to the door. There was dirt all over his face but he looked happy. "Come in," she said.

Hans looked over his shoulder and smiled, then turned back to Krystal.

"Come, Hans," she said.

He stood there. "Bitch," he said.

Krystal stepped backwards. She shook her head. "No," she said. "No no no. Don't say that. Come, sweet boy." She held out her arms.

"Bitch," he said again.

"Oh!" Krystal said. Her hand went to her mouth. Then she pushed open the door and walked up to Hans and slapped him across the face, something she had never done before. She slapped him hard. He sat down and looked up at her. Krystal took a flat board from the pile of scrap and turned toward the three men on the bench. They were watching her from under their big hats. "Who did that?" she said. "Who taught him that word?" When they didn't answer she started toward the bench, reviling them in German, using words she had never used before. They stood and backed away from her. Hans began to cry. Krystal turned on him. "Be quiet!" she said. He whimpered once and was still.

Krystal turned back to the men. "Who taught him that word?"

"It wasn't me," one of them said.

The other two just stood there.

"Shame," Krystal said. She looked at them, then walked over to the car. She kicked the boots aside. Holding the board with both hands, she swung it as hard as she could across the bare feet sticking out of the window. The man inside screamed. Krystal hit his feet again and he pulled them back.

"Get out," she said. "Out, out, out!"

The man who'd been sleeping inside, the one called Webb, scrambled out the other door and hopped from foot

to foot toward the building. He had left his hat in the car.
As he danced over the hot sand his hair flapped up and
down like a wing. He stopped in the shade and looked
back, still shifting from foot to foot. He kept his eyes on
Krystal. So did Hans, sitting by the door. So did the men
near the bench. They were all watching to see what she
would do next.

So, Krystal thought. She flung the board away, and one
of the men flinched. Krystal almost smiled. She thought,
How angry I must look, how angry I am, and then her
anger left her. She tried to keep it, but it was gone the
moment she knew it was there.

She shaded her eyes and looked around her. The distant
mountains cast long shadows into the desert. The desert
was empty and still. Nothing moved but Hope, walking
toward them with the gun over her shoulder. As she drew
near Krystal waved, and Hope raised her arms. A rabbit
hung from each hand, swinging by its ears.

OUR STORY
BEGINS

The fog blew in early again. This was the tenth straight day of it. The waiters and waitresses gathered along the window to watch, and Charlie pushed his cart across the dining room so that he could watch with them as he filled the water glasses. Boats were beating in ahead of the fog, which loomed behind them like a tall rolling breaker. Gulls glided from the sky to the pylons along the wharf, where they shook out their feathers and rocked from side to side and glared at the tourists passing by.

The fog covered the stanchions of the bridge. The bridge appeared to be floating free as the fog billowed into the harbor and began to overtake the boats. One by one they were swallowed up in it.

"Now that's what I call hairy," one of the waiters said. "You couldn't get me out there for love or money."

A waitress said something and the rest of them laughed.

"Nice talk," the waiter said.

The maître d' came out of the kitchen and snapped his fingers. "Busboy!" he called. One of the waitresses turned and looked at Charlie, who put down the pitcher he was pouring from and pushed his cart back across the dining room to its assigned place. For the next half hour, until the first customer came in, Charlie folded napkins and laid out squares of butter in little bowls filled with crushed ice, and thought of the things he would do to the maître d' if he ever got the maître d' in his power.

But this was a diversion; he didn't really hate the maître d'. He hated his meaningless work and his fear of being fired from it, and most of all he hated being called a busboy because being called a busboy made it harder for him to think of himself as a man, which he was just learning to do.

Only a few tourists came into the restaurant that night. All of them were alone, and plainly disappointed. They sat by themselves, across from their shopping bags, and stared morosely in the direction of the Golden Gate though there was nothing to see but the fog pressing up against the windows and greasy drops of water running down the glass. Like most people who ate alone they ordered the bargain items, scampi or cod or the Cap'n's Plate, and maybe a small carafe of the house wine. The waiters neglected them. The tourists dawdled over their food, overtipped the waiters, and left more deeply sunk in disappointment than before.

At nine o'clock the maître d' sent all but three of the waiters home, then went home himself. Charlie hoped he'd be given the nod too, but he was left standing by his cart, where he folded more napkins and replaced the ice as it melted in the water glasses and under the squares of butter. The three waiters kept going back to the storeroom to smoke dope. By the time the restaurant closed they were so wrecked they could hardly stand.

Charlie started home the long way, up Columbus Avenue, because Columbus Avenue had the brightest streetlights. But in this fog the lights were only a presence, a milky blotch here and there in the vapor above. Charlie walked slowly and kept to the walls. He met no one on his way;

but once, as he paused to wipe the dampness from his face, he heard strange ticking steps behind him and turned to see a three-legged dog appear out of the mist. It moved past in a series of lurches and was gone. "Christ," Charlie said. Then he laughed to himself, but the sound was unconvincing and he decided to get off the street for a while.

Just around the corner on Vallejo there was a coffeehouse where Charlie sometimes went on his nights off. Jack Kerouac had mentioned this particular coffeehouse in *The Subterraneans*. These days the patrons were mostly Italian people who came to listen to the jukebox, which was filled with music from Italian operas, but Charlie always looked up when someone came in the door; it might be Ginsberg or Corso, stopping by for old times' sake. He liked sitting there with an open book on the table, listening to music that he thought of as being classical. He liked to imagine that the rude, sluggish woman who brought him his cappuccino had once been Neil Cassady's lover. It was possible.

When Charlie came into the coffeehouse the only other customers were four old men sitting by the door. He took a table across the room. Someone had left an Italian movie magazine on the chair next to his. Charlie looked through the photographs, keeping time with his fingers to "The Anvil Chorus" while the waitress made up his cappuccino. The coffee machine hissed as she worked the handle. The room filled with the sweet smell of coffee. Charlie also caught the smell of fish and realized that it came from him, that he was reeking of it. His fingers fell still on the table.

Charlie paid the waitress when she served him. He intended to drink up and get out. While he was waiting for the coffee to cool, a woman came in the door with two men. They looked around, held a conference, and finally sat down at the table next to Charlie's. As soon as they were seated they began to talk without regard for whether Charlie could hear them. He listened, and after a time he began to glance over at them. Either they didn't notice or they didn't care. They were indifferent to his presence.

Charlie gathered from their conversation that they were members of a church choir, making the rounds after choir practice. The woman's name was Audrey. Her lipstick was smeared, making her mouth look a little crooked. She had a sharp face with thick black brows that she raised skeptically whenever her husband spoke. Audrey's husband was tall and heavy. He shifted constantly, scraping his chair as he did so, and moved his hat back and forth from one knee to the other. Big as he was, the green suit he wore fitted him perfectly. His name was Truman, and the other man's name was George. George had a calm, reedy voice that he enjoyed using; Charlie could see him listening to it as he talked. He was a teacher of some kind, which did not surprise Charlie. George looked to him like the young professors he'd had during his three years of college: rimless spectacles, turtleneck sweater, the ghost of a smile always on his lips. But George wasn't really young. His thick hair, parted in the middle, had begun to turn grey.

No — it seemed that only Audrey and George sang in the choir. They were telling Truman about a trip the choir had just made to Los Angeles, to a festival of choirs. Truman looked from his wife to George as each of them spoke, and shook his head as they described the sorry characters of the other members of the choir and the eccentricities of the choir director.

"Of course Father Wes is nothing compared to Monsignor Strauss," George said. "Monsignor Strauss was positively certifiable."

"Strauss?" Truman said. "Which one is Strauss? The only Strauss I know is Johann." Truman looked at his wife and laughed.

"Forgive me," George said. "I was being cryptic. George sometimes forgets the basics. When you've met someone like Monsignor Strauss, you naturally assume that everyone else has heard of him. The monsignor was our director for five years, prior to Father Wes's tenure. He got religion and left for the subcontinent just before Audrey joined us, so of course you wouldn't recognize the name."

"The subcontinent," Truman said. "What's that? Atlantis?"

"For God's sake, Truman," Audrey said. "Sometimes you embarrass me."

"India," George said. "Calcutta. Mother Teresa and all that."

Audrey put her hand on George's arm. "George," she said, "tell Truman that marvelous story you told me about Monsignor Strauss and the Filipino."

George smiled to himself. "Ah yes," he said. "Miguel. That's a long story, Audrey. Perhaps another night would be better."

"Oh no," Audrey said. "Tonight would be perfect."

Truman said, "If it's that long . . ."

"It's not," Audrey said. She knocked on the table with her knuckles. "Tell the story, George."

George looked over at Truman and shrugged. "Don't blame George," he said. He drank off the last of his brandy. "All right then. Our story begins. Monsignor Strauss had some money from somewhere, and every year he made a journey to points exotic. When he came home he always had some unusual souvenir that he'd picked up on his travels. From Argentina he brought everyone seeds which grew into plants whose flowers smelled like, excuse me, *merde*. He got them in an Argentine joke shop, if you can imagine such a thing. When he came back from Kenya he smuggled in a lizard that could pick off flies with its tongue from a distance of six feet. The monsignor carried this lizard around on his finger and whenever a fly came within range he would say, 'Watch this!' and aim the lizard like a pistol, and *poof* — no more fly."

Audrey pointed her finger at Truman and said, "Poof." Truman just looked at her. "I need another drink," Audrey said, and signaled the waitress.

George ran his finger around the rim of his snifter. "After the lizard," he said, "there was a large Australian rodent that ended up in the zoo, and after the rodent came a nineteen-year-old human being from the Philippines. His name was Miguel Lopez de Constanza, and he was a cab driver from Manila the monsignor had hired as a chauffeur during his stay there and taken a liking to. When the monsignor got back he pulled some strings at Immigration, and a few weeks later Miguel showed up. He spoke no English, really — only a few buzz words for tourists in Manila. The first month or so he stayed with Monsignor Strauss in the rectory, then he found a room in the Hotel Overland and moved in there."

"The Hotel Overland," Truman said. "That's that druggy hangout on upper Grant."

"The Hotel Overdose," Audrey said. When Truman looked at her she said, "That's what they call it."

"You seem to be up on all the nomenclature," Truman said.

The waitress came with their drinks. When her tray was empty she stood behind Truman and began to write in a notebook she carried. Charlie hoped she wouldn't come over to his table. He did not want the others to notice him. They would guess that he'd been listening to them, and they might not like it. They might stop talking. But the waitress finished making her entries and moved back to the bar without a glance at Charlie.

The old men by the door were arguing in Italian. The window above them was all steamed up, and Charlie could feel the closeness of the fog outside. The jukebox glowed in the corner. The song that was playing ended abruptly, the machinery whirred, and "The Anvil Chorus" came on again.

"So why the Hotel Overland?" Truman asked.

"Truman prefers the Fairmont," Audrey said. "Truman thinks everyone should stay at the Fairmont."

"Miguel had no money," George said. "Only what the monsignor gave him. The idea was that he would stay there just long enough to learn English and pick up a trade. Then he could get a job. Take care of himself."

"Sounds reasonable," Truman said.

Audrey laughed. "Truman, you slay me. That is *exactly* what I thought you would say. Now let's just turn things around for a minute. Let's say that for some reason you, Truman, find yourself in Manila dead broke. You don't know anybody, you don't understand anything anyone says, and you wind up in a hotel where people are sticking needles into themselves and nodding out on the stairs and setting their rooms on fire all the time. How much Spanish

are you going to learn living like that? What kind of trade
are you going to pick up? Get real," Audrey said. "That's
not a reasonable existence."

"San Francisco isn't Manila," Truman said. "Believe
me — I've been there. At least here you've got a chance.
And it isn't true that he didn't know anybody. What about
the monsignor?"

"Terrific," Audrey said. "A priest who walks around
with a lizard on his finger. Great friend. Or, as you would
say, great connection."

"I have never, to my knowledge, used the word *connection* in that way," Truman said.

George had been staring into his brandy snifter, which
he held cupped in both hands. He looked up at Audrey.
"Actually," he said, "Miguel was not entirely at a loss. In
fact he managed pretty well for a time. Monsignor Strauss
got him into a training course for mechanics at the
Porsche-Audi place on Van Ness, and he picked up English
at a terrific rate. It's amazing, isn't it, what one can do if
one has no choice." George rolled the snifter back and
forth between his palms. "The druggies left him completely alone, incredible as that may seem. No hassles in
the hallways, nothing. It was as if Miguel lived in a different
dimension from them, and in a way he did. He went to
Mass every day, and sang in the choir. That's where I made
his acquaintance. Miguel had a gorgeous baritone, truly
gorgeous. He was extremely proud of his voice. He was
proud of his body, too. Ate precisely so much of this, so
much of that. Did elaborate exercises every day. He even
gave himself facial massages to keep from getting a double
chin."

"There you are," Truman said to Audrey. "There is

such a thing as character." When she didn't answer he
added, "What I'm getting at is that people are not neces-
sarily limited by their circumstances."

"I know what you're getting at," Audrey said. "The
story isn't over yet."

Truman moved his hat from his knee to the table. He
folded his arms across his chest. "I've got a full day ahead
of me," he said to Audrey. She nodded but did not look
at him.

George took a sip of his brandy. He closed his eyes afterwards and ran the tip of his tongue around his lips. Then
he lowered his head again and stared back into the snifter.
"Miguel met a woman," he said, "as do we all. Her name
was Senga. My guess is that she had originally been called
Agnes, and that she turned her name around in hopes of
making herself more interesting to people of the male
persuasion. Senga was older than Miguel by at least ten
years, maybe more. She had a daughter in, I believe, fifth
grade. Senga was a finance officer at B of A. I don't remember how they met. They went out for a while, then Senga
broke it off. I suppose it was a casual thing for her, but
for Miguel it was serious. He worshiped Senga, and I use
that word advisedly. He set up a little shrine to her in his
room. A high school graduation picture of Senga sur-
rounded by different objects that she had worn or used.
Combs. Handkerchiefs. Empty perfume bottles. A whole
pile of things. How he got them I have no idea — whether
she gave them to him or whether he just took them. The
odd thing is, he only went out with her a few times. I very
much doubt that they ever reached the point of sleeping
together."

"They didn't," Truman said.

George looked up at him.

"If he'd slept with her," Truman said, "he wouldn't have built a shrine to her."

Audrey shook her head. "Pure Truman," she said. "Vintage Truman."

He patted her arm. "No offense," he told her.

"Be that as it may," George said, "Miguel wouldn't give up, and that's what caused all the trouble. First he wrote her letters, long mushy letters in broken English. He gave me one to read through for spelling and so on, but it was utterly hopeless. All fragments and run-ons. No paragraphs. I just gave it back after a few days and said it was fine. Miguel thought that the letters would bring Senga around, but she never answered and after a while he began calling her at all hours. She wouldn't talk to him. As soon as she heard his voice she hung up. Eventually she got an unlisted number. She wouldn't talk to Miguel, but Miguel thought that she would listen to yours truly. He wanted me to go down to B of A and plead his cause. Act as a kind of character witness. Which, after some reflection, I agreed to do."

"Oho," Truman said. "The plot thickens. Enter Miles Standish."

"I *knew* you would say that," Audrey said. She finished her drink and looked around, but the waitress was sitting at the bar with her back to the room, smoking a cigarette.

George took his glasses off, held them up to the light, and put them on again. "So," he said, "George sallies forth to meet Senga. Senga — doesn't it make you think of a jungle queen, that name? Flashing eyes, dagger at the hip, breasts bulging over a leopard-skin halter? Such was not the case.

This Senga was still an Agnes. Thin. Businesslike. And *very* grouchy. No sooner did I mention Miguel's name than I was shown the door, with a message for Miguel: if he bothered her again she would set the police on him.

" 'Set the police on him.' Those were her words, and she meant them. A week or so later Miguel followed her home from work and she forthwith got a lawyer on the case. The upshot of it was that Miguel had to sign a paper saying that he understood he would be arrested if he wrote, called, or followed Senga again. He signed, but with his fingers crossed, as it were. He told me, 'Horhay, I sign — but I do not accept.' 'Nobly spoken,' I told him, 'but you'd damn well better accept or that woman will have you locked up.' Miguel said that prison did not frighten him, that in his country all the best people were in prison. Sure enough, a few days later he followed Senga home again and she did it — she had him locked up."

"Poor kid," Audrey said.

Truman had been trying to get the attention of the waitress, who wouldn't look at him. He turned to Audrey. "What do you mean, 'Poor kid'? What about the girl? Senga? She's trying to hold down a job and feed her daughter and meanwhile she has this Filipino stalking her all over the city. If you want to feel sorry for someone, feel sorry for her."

"I do," Audrey said.

"All right then." Truman looked back toward the waitress again, and as he did so Audrey picked up George's snifter and took a drink from it. George smiled at her. "What's wrong with that woman?" Truman said. He shook his head. "I give up."

"George, go on," Audrey said.

George nodded. "In brief," he said, "it was a serious mess. *Très sérieux*. They set bail at twenty thousand dollars, which Monsignor Strauss could not raise. Nor, it goes without saying, could yours truly. So Miguel remained in jail. Senga's lawyer was out for blood, and he got Immigration into the act. They were threatening to revoke Miguel's visa and throw him out of the country. Monsignor Strauss finally got him off, but it was, as the Duke said, a damn close-run thing. It turned out that Senga was going to be transferred to Portland in a month or so, and the monsignor persuaded her to drop charges with the understanding that Miguel would not come within ten miles of the city limits as long as she lived there. Until she left, Miguel would stay with Monsignor Strauss at the rectory, under his personal supervision. The monsignor also agreed to pay Senga for her lawyer's fees, which were outrageous. Absolutely outrageous."

"So what was the bottom line?" Truman asked.

"Simplicity itself," George said. "If Miguel messed up, they'd throw him on the first plane to Manila."

"Sounds illegal," Truman said.

"Perhaps. But that was the arrangement."

A new song began on the jukebox. The men by the door stopped arguing, and each of them seemed all at once to draw into himself.

"Listen," Audrey said. "It's him. Caruso."

The record was worn and gave the effect of static behind Caruso's voice. The music coming through the static made Charlie think of the cultural broadcasts from Europe his parents had listened to so gravely when he was a boy. At times Caruso's voice was almost lost, and then it would swell again. The old men were still. One of them began to weep. The tears fell freely from his open eyes, down his shining cheeks.

"So that was Caruso," Truman said when it ended. "I always wondered what all the fuss was about. Now I know. That's what I call singing." Truman took out his wallet and put some money on the table. He examined the money left in the wallet before putting it away. "Ready?" he said to Audrey.

"No," Audrey said. "Finish the story, George."

George took his glasses off and laid them next to his snifter. He rubbed his eyes. "All right," he said. "Back to Miguel. As per the agreement, he lived in the rectory until Senga moved to Portland. Behaved himself, too. No letters, no calls, no following her around. In his pajamas every night by ten. Then Senga left town and Miguel went back to his room at the Overland. For a while there he looked pretty desperate, but after a few weeks he seemed to come out of it.

"I say 'seemed.' There was in fact more going on than met the eye. My eye, anyway. One night I am sitting at home and listening, believe it or not, to *Tristan*, when the telephone rings. At first no one says anything; then this voice comes on the line whispering, "Help me, Horhay, help me," and of course I know who it is. He says he needs to see me right away. No explanation. He doesn't even tell me where he is. I just have to assume he's at the Overland, and that's where I find him, in the lobby."

George gave a little laugh. "Actually," he said, "I almost missed him. His face was all bandaged up, from his nose to the top of his forehead. If I hadn't been looking for him I never would have recognized him. Never. He was sitting there with his suitcases all around him and a white cane across his knees. When I made my presence known to him he said, "Horhay, I am blind." How, I asked him, had this come to pass? He would not say. Instead he gave me a piece of paper with a telephone number on it and asked me to call Senga and tell her that he had gone blind, and that he would be arriving in Portland by Trailways at eleven o'clock the next morning."

"Great Scott," Truman said. "He was faking it, wasn't he? I mean he wasn't really blind, was he?"

"Now that is an interesting question," George said. "Because, while I would have to say that Miguel was not really blind, I would also have to say that he was not really faking it, either. But to go on. Senga was unmoved. She instructed me to tell Miguel that not she but the police would be waiting to meet his bus. Miguel didn't believe her. 'Horhay,' he said, 'she will be there,' and that was that. End of discussion."

"Did he go?" Truman asked.

"Of course he went," Audrey said. "He loved her."

George nodded. "I put him on the bus myself. Led him to his seat, in fact."

"So he still had the bandages on," Truman said.

"Oh yes. Yes, he still had them on."

"But that's a twelve-, thirteen-hour ride. If there wasn't anything wrong with his eyes, why didn't he just take the bandages off and put them on again when the bus reached Portland?"

Audrey put her hand on Truman's. "Truman," she said. "We have to talk about something."

"I don't get it," Truman went on. "Why would he travel blind like that? Why would he go all that way in the dark?"

"Truman, listen," Audrey said. But when Truman

turned to her she took her hand away from his and looked across the table at George. George's eyes were closed. His fingers were folded together as if in prayer.

"George," Audrey said. "Please. I can't."

George opened his eyes.

"Tell him," Audrey said.

Truman looked back and forth between them. "Now just wait a minute," he said.

"I'm sorry," George said. "This is not easy for me."

Truman was staring at Audrey. "Hey," he said.

She pushed her empty glass back and forth. "We have to talk," she said.

He brought his face close to hers. "Do you think that just because I make a lot of money I don't have feelings?"

"We have to talk," she repeated.

"Indeed," George said.

The three of them sat there for a while. Then Truman said, "This takes the cake," and put his hat on. A few minutes later they all got up and left the coffeehouse.

The waitress sat by herself at the bar, motionless except when she raised her head to blow smoke at the ceiling. Over by the door the Italians were throwing dice for toothpicks. "The Anvil Chorus" was playing on the jukebox. It was the first piece of classical music Charlie had heard often enough to get sick of, and he was sick of it now. He closed the magazine he'd been pretending to read, dropped it on the table, and went outside.

It was still foggy, and colder than before. Charlie's father had warned him about moving here in the middle of the summer. He had even quoted Mark Twain at Charlie, to the effect that the coldest winter Mark Twain ever endured was the summer he spent in San Francisco. This had been a particularly bad one; even the natives said so. In truth it was beginning to get to Charlie. But he had not admitted this to his father, any more than he had admitted that his job was wearing him out and paying him barely enough to keep alive on, or that the friends he wrote home about did not exist, or that the editors to whom he'd submitted his novel had sent it back without comment — all but one, who had scrawled in pencil across the title page, "Are you kidding?"

Charlie's room was on Broadway, at the crest of the hill. The hill was so steep they'd had to carve steps into the sidewalk and block the street with a cement wall because of the cars that had lost their brakes going down. Sometimes, at night, Charlie would sit on that wall and look out over the lights of North Beach and think of all the writers out there, bent over their desks, steadily filling pages with well-chosen words. He thought of these writers gathering together in the small hours to drink wine, and read each other's work, and talk about the things that weighed on their hearts. These were the brilliant men and women, the deep conversations Charlie wrote home about.

He was close to giving up. He didn't even know how close to giving up he was until he walked out of the coffeehouse that night and felt himself deciding that he would go on after all. He stood there and listened to the foghorn blowing out upon the Bay. The sadness of that sound, the idea of himself stopping to hear it, the thickness of the fog all gave him pleasure.

Charlie heard violins behind him as the coffeehouse door opened; then it banged shut and the violins were gone. A deep voice said something in Italian. A higher voice answered, and the two voices floated away together down the street.

Charlie turned and started up the hill, picking his way past lampposts that glistened with running beads of water, past sweating walls and dim windows. A Chinese woman appeared beside him. She held before her a lobster that was waving its pincers back and forth as if conducting music. The woman hurried past and vanished. The hill began to steepen under Charlie's feet. He stopped to catch his breath, and listened again to the foghorn. He knew that somewhere out there a boat was making its way home in spite of the solemn warning, and as he walked on Charlie imagined himself kneeling in the prow of that boat, lamp in hand, intent on the light shining just before him. All distraction gone. Too watchful to be afraid. Tongue wetting the lips and eyes wide open, ready to call out in this shifting fog where at any moment anything might be revealed.

LEVIATHAN

On her thirtieth birthday Ted threw a surprise party for Helen. It was a small party — Mitch and Bliss were the only guests. They'd chipped in with Ted and bought Helen three grams of white-out blizzard that lasted the whole night and on into the next morning. When it got light enough everyone went for a swim in the court-yard pool. Then Ted took Mitch up to the sauna on the fifth floor while Helen and Bliss put together a monster omelet.

"So how does it feel," Bliss said, "being thirty?" The ash fell off her cigarette into the eggs. She stared at the ash for a moment, then stirred it in. "Mitch had his fortieth last month and totally freaked. He did so much Maalox he started to taste like chalk. I thought he was going to start freebasing it or something."

"Mitch is *forty?*" Helen said.

Bliss looked over at her. "That's classified information, okay?"

Helen shook her head. "Incredible. He looks about twenty-five, maybe twenty-seven at the absolute most." She watched Bliss crumble bacon into the bowl. "Oh God," she said, "I don't believe it. He had a face lift."

Bliss closed her eyes and leaned against the counter. "I shouldn't have told you. Please don't say anything," she murmured hopelessly.

When Mitch and Ted came back from the sauna they all

had another toot, and Ted gave Helen the mirror to lick.
He said he'd never seen three grams disappear so fast.
Afterwards Helen served up the omelet while Ted tried
to find something on the TV. He kept flipping the dial
until it drove everyone crazy, looking for Roadrunner
cartoons, then he gave up and tuned in on the last part
of a movie about the Bataan Death March. They didn't
watch it for very long though because Bliss started to cry.
Ted switched over to an inspirational program but Bliss
kept crying and began to hyperventilate. "Come on, everyone," said Mitch. "Love circle." Ted and Mitch went over
to Bliss and put their arms around her while Helen
watched them from the sofa, sipping espresso from a cup
as blue and dainty as a robin's egg — the last of a set her
grandmother had brought from the old country. Helen
would have hugged Bliss too but there wasn't really any
point; Bliss pulled this stunt almost every time she got
herself a noseful, and it just had to run its course.

When Helen finished her espresso she gathered the
plates and carried them out to the kitchen. She scattered
leftover toast into the courtyard below, and watched the
squirrels carry it away as she scoured the dishes and
listened to the proceedings in the next room. This time it
was Ted who talked Bliss down. "You're beautiful," he
kept telling her. It was the same thing he always said to
Helen when she felt depressed, and she was beginning to
feel depressed right now.

I need more fuel, Helen thought. She ducked into the
bedroom and did a couple of lines from Ted's private
stash, which she had discovered while searching for
matches in the closet. Afterwards she looked at herself in
the mirror. Her eyes were bright. They seemed lit from
within and that was how Helen felt, as if there were a

column of cool white light pouring from her head to her feet like a waterfall. She put on a pair of sunglasses so nobody would notice and went back to the kitchen.

Mitch was standing at the counter, rolling a bone. "How's the birthday girl?" he asked without looking up.

"Ready for the next one," Helen said. "How about you?"

"Hey, bring it on," Mitch answered.

Helen smiled at him. At that moment she came close to letting him know she knew, but she held back. Mitch was good people and so was Bliss when you could get her off the subject of Mary Kay. Helen didn't want to make trouble between them. All the same, Helen knew that someday she wasn't going to be able to stop herself from giving Mitch the business. It just had to happen. And Helen knew that Bliss knew. But she hadn't done it this morning and she felt good about that.

Mitch held up the joint. "Taste?"

Helen shook her head. She glanced over her shoulder toward the living room. "What's the story on Bliss?" she asked. "All bummed out over World War Two? Ted should have known that movie would set her off."

Mitch picked a sliver of weed from his lower lip. "Her ex is threatening to move back to Boston. Which means she won't get to see her kids except during the summer, and that's only if we can put together the scratch to fly them here and back. It's tough. Really tough."

"I guess," Helen said. She dried her hands and hung the towel on the refrigerator door. "Still, Bliss should have thought about that when she took a walk on them, right?"

Mitch turned and started out of the kitchen.

"Sorry," Helen called after him. "I wasn't thinking."

"Yes you were," Mitch said, and left her there.

Oh, hell, she thought. She decided she needed another line but made no move to get it. Helen stood where she was, looking down at the pool through the window above the sink. The manager's Afghan dog was lapping water from the shallow end, legs braced in the trough that ran around the pool. The two British Air stewards from down the hall were bathing their white bodies in the morning sunshine, both wearing blue swimsuits. The redheaded girl from upstairs was floating on an air mattress. Helen could see the long shadow of the air mattress glide along the bottom of the pool like something stalking her.

Helen heard Ted say, "Jesus, Bliss, I can understand that. Everybody has those feelings. You can't always beat them down." Bliss answered him in a voice so soft that Helen gave up trying to hear; it was hardly more than a sigh. She poured herself a glass of Chablis and joined the others in the living room. They were all sitting cross-legged on the floor. Helen caught Mitch's eye and mouthed the word *sorry*. He stared at her, then nodded.

"I've done worse things than that," Ted was saying. "I'll bet Mitch has, too."

"Plenty worse," Mitch said.

"Worse than what?" Helen asked.

"It's awful." Bliss looked down at her hands. "I'd be embarrassed to tell you." She was all cried out now, Helen could see that. Her eyes were heavy-lidded and serene, her cheeks flushed, and a little smile played over her swollen lips.

"It couldn't be that bad," Helen said.

Ted leaned forward. He still had on the bathrobe he'd worn to the sauna and it fell open almost to his waist, as Helen knew he intended it to do. His chest was hard-looking from the Nautilus machine in the basement, and dark from their trip to Mazatlán. Helen had to admit it, he looked great. She didn't understand why he had to be so obvious and crass, but he got what he wanted: she stared at him and so did Bliss.

"Bliss, it *isn't* that bad," Ted went on. "It's just one of those things." He turned to Helen. "Bliss's little girl came down with tonsillitis last month and Bliss never got it together to go see her in the hospital."

"I can't deal with hospitals," Bliss said. "The minute I set foot inside of one my stomach starts doing flips. But still. When I think of her all alone in there."

Mitch took Bliss's hands in his and looked right at her until she met his gaze. "It's over," he said. "The operation's over and Lisa's out of the hospital and she's all right. Say it, Bliss. *She's all right.*"

"She's all right," Bliss said.

"Again."

"She's all right," Bliss repeated.

"Okay. Now believe it." Mitch put her hands together and rubbed them gently between his palms. "We've built up this big myth about kids being helpless and vulnerable and so on because it makes us feel important. We think we're playing some heavy role just because we're parents. We don't give kids any credit at all. Kids are tough little monkeys. Kids are survivors."

Bliss smiled.

"But I don't know," Mitch said. He let go of Bliss's hands and leaned back. "What I said just then is probably complete bullshit. Everything I say these days sounds like bullshit."

"We've all done worse things," Ted told Bliss. He looked over at Helen. When Helen saw that he was waiting for her to agree with him she tried to think of something to say, but finally just nodded. Ted kept looking at her. "What have you got those things on for?" he asked.

"The light hurts my eyes."

"Then close the curtains." He reached across to Helen and lifted the sunglasses away from her face. "There," he said. He cupped her chin in one hand and with the other brushed her hair back from her forehead. "Isn't she something?"

"She'll do," Mitch said.

Ted stroked Helen's cheek with the back of his hand. "I'd kill for that face."

Bliss was studying Helen. "So lovely," she said in a solemn, wistful voice.

Helen laughed. She got up and drew the curtains shut. Spangles of light glittered in the fabric. She moved across the dim room to the dining nook and brought back a candle from the table there. Ted lit the candle and for a few moments they silently watched the flame. Then, in a thoughtful tone that seemed part of the silence, Mitch began to speak.

"It's true that we've all done things we're ashamed of. I just wish I'd done more of them. I'm serious," he said when Ted laughed. "I wish I'd raised more hell and made more mistakes, real mistakes, where you actually do something wrong instead of just let yourself drift into things you don't like. Sometimes I look around and I think, *Hey — what happened*? No reflection on you," he said to Bliss.

She seemed puzzled.

"Forget it," Mitch told her. "All I'm saying is that looking out for the other fellow and being nice all the time is a bunch of crap."

"But you *are* nice," Bliss said.

Mitch nodded. "I know," he said bitterly. "I'm working on it. It gets you exactly nowhere."

"Amen," said Ted.

"Case in point," Mitch went on. "I used to paralegal with this guy in the city and he decided that he couldn't live without some girl he was seeing. So he told his wife and of course she threw him out. Then the girl changed her mind. She didn't even tell him why. We used to eat lunch together and he would give me the latest installment and I swear to God it was enough to break your heart. He wanted to get back together with his family but his wife couldn't make up her mind whether to take him. One minute she'd say yes, the next minute she'd say no. Meanwhile he was living in this ratbag on Post Street. All he had in there was lawn furniture. I don't know, I just felt sorry for him. So I told him he could move in with us until things got straightened out."

"I can feel this one coming," Helen said.

Mitch stared at the candle. "His name was Raphael. Like the angel. He was creative and good-looking and there was a nice aura around him. I guess I wanted to be his friend. But he turned out to be completely bad news. In the nine months he stayed with us he never once washed a glass or emptied an ashtray. He ran up hundreds of dollars worth of calls on our phone bill and didn't pay for them. He wrecked my car. He stole things from me. He even put the moves on my wife."

"Classic," Helen said.

"You know what I did about it?" Mitch asked. "I'll tell you. Nothing. I never said a word to him about any of it. By the time he left, my wife couldn't stand the sight of me. Beginning of the end."

"What a depressing story," Helen said.

"I should have killed him," Mitch said. "I might have regretted it later on but at least I could say I *did* something."

"You're too sweet," Bliss told him.

"I know," Mitch said. "But I wish I had, anyway. Sometimes it's better to do something really horrendous than to let things slide."

Ted clapped his hands. "Hear, hear. You're on the right track, Mitch. All you need is a few pointers, and old Ted is just the man to give them to you. Because where horrendous is concerned I'm the expert. You might say that I'm the king of horrendous."

Helen held up her empty glass. "Anybody want anything?"

"Put on your crash helmets," Ted went on. "You are about to hear my absolute bottom-line confession. The Worst Story Ever Told."

"No thanks," said Helen.

He peered at her. "What do you mean, 'No thanks.' Who's asking permission?"

"I wouldn't mind hearing it," Mitch said.

"Well I would." Helen stood and looked down at Ted. "It's my birthday party, remember? I just don't feel like sitting around and listening to you talk about what a crud you are. It's a downer."

"That's right," Bliss said. "Helen's the birthday girl. She gets to choose. Right, Ted?"

"I know what," Helen said. "Why don't you tell us something good you did? The thing you're most proud of."

Mitch burst out laughing. Ted grinned and punched him in the arm.

"I mean it," Helen said.

"Helen gets to choose," Bliss repeated. She patted the floor beside her and Helen sat down again. "All right," Bliss said. "We're listening."

Ted looked from Bliss to Helen. "I'll do it if you will," he said. "But you have to go first."

"That's not fair," Helen said.

"Sounds fair to me," said Mitch. "It was your idea."

Bliss smiled at Helen. "This is fun."

Before Helen began, she sent Ted out to the kitchen for more wine. Mitch did some sit-ups to get his blood moving again. Bliss sat behind Helen and let down Helen's hair. "I could show you something for this dryness," she said. She combed Helen's hair with her fingers, then started to brush it, counting off the strokes in a breathy whisper until Ted came back with the jug.

They all had a drink.

"Ready and waiting," Ted told Helen. He lay back on the sofa and clasped his hands behind his head.

"One of my mother's friends had a boy with Down's syndrome," Helen began. "Actually, three or four of her friends had kids with problems like that. One of my aunts, too. They were all good Catholics and they didn't think anything about having babies right into their forties. This was before Vatican Two and the pill and all that — before everything got watered down.

"Anyway, Tom wasn't really a boy. He was older than me by a couple of years, and a lot bigger. But he seemed like a boy — very sweet, very gentle, very happy."

Bliss stopped the brush in midstroke and said, "You're going to make me cry again."

"I used to take care of Tom sometimes when I was in

high school. I was into a serious good-works routine back
then. I wanted to be a saint. Honestly, I really did. At
night, before I went to sleep, I used to put my fingers under
my chin like I was praying and smile in this really holy
way that I practiced all the time in front of the mirror.
Then if they found me dead in the morning they would
think that I'd gone straight to heaven — that I was smiling
at the angels coming to get me. At one point I even
thought of becoming a nun."

Bliss laughed. "I can just see you in a habit — Sister
Morphine. You'd have lasted about two hours."

Helen turned and looked at Bliss in a speculative way.
"It's not something I expect you to understand," she said,
"but if I had gone in I would have stayed in. To me, a
vow is a vow." She turned away again. "Like I said, I
started out taking care of Tom as a kind of beatitude
number, but after a while I got to look forward to it. Tom
was fun to be with. And he really loved me. He even
named one of his hamsters after me. We were both crazy
about animals, so we would usually go to the zoo or I
would take him to this stable out in Marin that had free
riding lessons for special kids. That was what they called
them, instead of handicapped or retarded — special."

"Beautiful," Mitch said.

"Don't get too choked up," Helen told him. "The story
isn't over yet." She took a sip of her wine. "So. After I
started college I didn't get home all that much, but whenever I did I'd stop by and get Tom and we'd go somewhere. Over to the Cliff House to look at the sea lions,
something like that. Then this one day I got a real brain-
storm. I thought, Hey, why not go whale-watching? Tom
had whale posters all over his bedroom but he'd never seen

a real one, and neither had I. So I called up this outfit in Half Moon Bay and they said that it was getting toward the end of the season, but still worth a try. They were pretty sure we'd see something.

"Tom's mother wasn't too hot about the idea. She kept going on about the fact that he couldn't swim. But I brought her around, and the next morning Tom and I drove down and got on board the boat. It wasn't all that big. In fact it was a lot smaller than I thought it would be, and that made me a little nervous at first, but after we got under way I figured hell with it — they must know what they're doing. The boat rocked a little, but not dangerously. Tom loved it.

"We cruised around all morning and didn't see a thing. They would take us to different places and cut the engine and we would sit there, waiting for a whale to come along. I stopped caring. It was nice out on the water. We were with a good bunch of people and one of them fixed up a sort of fishing line for Tom to hang over the side while we waited. I just leaned back and got some sun. Smelled the good smells. Watched the seagulls. After an hour or so they would start the engine up again and go somewhere else and do the same thing. This happened three or four times. Everybody was kidding the guide about it, threatening to make him walk the plank and so on. Then, right out of nowhere, this whale came up beside us.

"He was just suddenly *there*. All this water running off his back. This unbelievably rancid smell all around him. Covered with barnacles and shells and long strings of seaweed trailing off him. Big. Maybe half again as long as the boat we were in." Helen shook her head. "You just can't imagine how big he was. He started making passes at the boat, and every time he did it we'd pitch and roll and take on about five hundred gallons of water. We were falling all over each other. At first everyone laughed and whooped it up, but after a while it started to get heavy."

"He was probably playing with you," Mitch said.

"That's what the guide told us the first couple of times it happened. Then he got scared too. I mean he went white as a sheet. You could tell he didn't know what was happening any better than the rest of us did. We have this idea that whales are supposed to be more civilized than people, smarter and friendlier and more together. Cute, even. But it wasn't like that. It was hostile."

"You probably got a bad one," Mitch said. "It sounds like he was bent out of shape about something. Maybe the Russians harpooned his mate."

"He was a monster," Helen said. "I mean that. He was hostile and huge and he stank. He was hideous, too. There were so many shells and barnacles on him that you could hardly see his skin. It looked as if he had armor on. He scraped the boat a couple of times and it made the most terrible sound, like people moaning under water. He'd swim ahead a ways and go under and you'd think Please God don't let him come back, and then the water would start to churn alongside the boat and there he'd be again. It was just terrifying. I've never been so afraid in my life. And then Tom started to lose it."

Bliss put the brush on the floor. Helen could feel her stillness and hear the sound of her breathing.

"He started to make these little noises," Helen said. "I'd never heard him do that before. Little mewing noises. The strange thing was, I hadn't even thought of Tom up to then. I'd completely forgotten about him. So it gave me a shock when I realized that he was sitting right next to me, scared half to death. At first I thought, Oh no, what if he goes berserk! He was so much bigger than me I wouldn't have been able to control him. Neither would anyone else. He was incredibly strong. If anyone had tried to hold him down he'd have thrown them off like a dog shakes off water. And then what?

"But the thing that worried me most was that Tom would get so confused and panicky that he'd jump overboard. In my mind I had a completely clear picture of him doing it."

"Me too," Mitch said. "I have the same picture. He did it, didn't he? He jumped in and you went after him and pulled him out."

Bliss said, "Ssshhh. Just listen, okay?"

"He didn't jump," Helen said. "He didn't go berserk, either. Here we come to the point of the story — Helen's Finest Hour. How did I get started on this, anyway? It's disgusting."

The candle hissed and flared. The flame was burning in a pool of wax. Helen watched it flare up twice more, and then it died. The room went grey.

· Bliss began to rub Helen's back. "Go on," she said.

"I just talked him down," Helen said. "You know, I put my arm around his shoulder and said, Hey, Tom, isn't this something! Look at that big old whale! Wow! Here he comes again, Tom, hold on! And then I'd laugh like crazy. I made like I was having the time of my life, and Tom fell for it. He calmed right down. Pretty soon after that the whale took off and we went back to shore. I don't know why I brought it up. It was just that even though I felt really afraid, I went ahead and acted as if I was flying high. I guess that's the thing I'm most proud of."

Helen rose up on her knees and stretched. "This happened nine years ago," she added.

"Thank you, Helen," Mitch said. "Thank you for sharing that with us. I know I sound phony but I mean it."

"You don't talk about yourself enough," Bliss said. Then she called, "Okay, Ted — it's your turn."

Ted did not answer.

Bliss called his name again.

"I think he's asleep," Mitch said. He moved closer to the sofa and looked at Ted. He nodded. "Dead to the world."

"Asleep," Helen said. "Oh, God."

Bliss hugged Helen from behind. "Mitch, come here," she said. "Love circle."

Helen pulled away. "No," she said.

"Why don't we wake him up?" Mitch suggested.

"Forget it," Helen told him. "Once Ted goes under he stays under. Nothing can bring him up. Watch." She went to the sofa, raised her hand, and slapped Ted across the face.

He groaned softly and turned over.

"See?" Helen said.

"What a slug," Bliss said.

"Don't you dare call him names," Helen told her. "Not in front of me, anyway. Ted is my husband. Forever and ever. I only did that to make a point."

Mitch said, "Helen, do you want to talk about this?"

"There's nothing to talk about," Helen answered. "I made my own bed." She hefted the jug of wine. "Who needs a refill?"

Mitch and Bliss looked at each other. "My energy level isn't too high," Bliss said.

Mitch nodded. "Mine's pretty low, too."

"Then we'll just have to bring it up," Helen said. She left the room and came back with three candles and a mirror. She screwed one of the candles into the holder and held a match to the wick. It sputtered, then caught. Helen felt the heat of the flame on her cheek. "There," she said, "that's more like it." Mitch and Bliss drew closer as Helen took a glass vial from her pocket and spilled the contents onto the mirror. She looked up at them and grinned.

"I don't believe this," Bliss said. "Where did you get it?"

Helen shrugged.

"That's a lot of toot," Mitch said.

"We'll just have to do our best," Helen said. "We've got all day."

Bliss looked at the mirror. "I really should go to work."

"Me too," Mitch said. He laughed, and Bliss laughed with him. They watched over Helen's shoulders as Helen bent down to sift the gleaming crystal. First she chopped it with a razor. Then she began to spread it out. Mitch and Bliss smiled up at her from the mirror, and Helen smiled back between them. Their faces were rosy with candlelight. They were the faces of three well-wishers, carolers, looking in at Helen through a window filling up with snow.

THE RICH
BROTHER

There were two brothers, Pete and Donald.

Pete, the older brother, was in real estate. He and his wife had a Century 21 franchise in Santa Cruz. Pete worked hard and made a lot of money, but not any more than he thought he deserved. He had two daughters, a sailboat, a house from which he could see a thin slice of the ocean, and friends doing well enough in their own lives not to wish bad luck on him. Donald, the younger brother, was still single. He lived alone, painted houses when he found the work, and got deeper in debt to Pete when he didn't.

No one would have taken them for brothers. Where Pete was stout and hearty and at home in the world, Donald was bony, grave, and obsessed with the fate of his soul. Over the years Donald had worn the images of two different Perfect Masters around his neck. Out of devotion to the second of these he entered an ashram in Berkeley, where he nearly died of undiagnosed hepatitis. By the time Pete finished paying the medical bills Donald had become a Christian. He drifted from church to church, then joined a pentecostal community that met somewhere in the Mission District to sing in tongues and swap prophecies.

Pete couldn't make sense of it. Their parents were both dead, but while they were alive neither of them had found it necessary to believe in anything. They managed to be decent people without making fools of themselves, and

Pete had the same ambition. He thought that the whole thing was an excuse for Donald to take himself seriously.

The trouble was that Donald couldn't content himself with worrying about his own soul. He had to worry about everyone else's, and especially Pete's. He handed down his judgments in ways that he seemed to consider subtle: through significant silence, innuendo, looks of mild despair that said, *Brother, what have you come to?* What Pete had come to, as far as he could tell, was prosperity. That was the real issue between them. Pete prospered and Donald did not prosper.

At the age of forty Pete took up sky diving. He made his first jump with two friends who'd started only a few months earlier and were already doing stunts. They were both coked to the gills when they jumped but Pete wanted to do it straight, at least the first time, and he was glad that he did. He would never have used the word *mystical*, but that was how Pete felt about the experience. Later he made the mistake of trying to describe it to Donald, who kept asking how much it cost and then acted appalled when Pete told him.

"At least I'm trying something new," Pete said. "At least I'm breaking the pattern."

Not long after that conversation Donald also broke the pattern, by going to live on a farm outside of Paso Robles. The farm was owned by several members of Donald's community, who had bought it and moved there with the idea of forming a family of faith. That was how Donald explained it in the first letter he sent. Every week Pete heard how happy Donald was, how "in the Lord." He told Pete that he was praying for him, he and the rest of Pete's brothers and sisters on the farm.

"I only have one brother," Pete wanted to answer, "and that's enough." But he kept this thought to himself.

In November the letters stopped. Pete didn't worry about this at first, but when he called Donald at Thanksgiving Donald was grim. He tried to sound upbeat but he didn't try hard enough to make it convincing. "Now listen," Pete said, "you don't have to stay in that place if you don't want to."

"I'll be all right," Donald answered.

"That's not the point. Being all right is not the point. If you don't like what's going on up there, then get out."

"I'm all right," Donald said again, more firmly. "I'm doing fine."

But he called Pete a week later and said that he was quitting the farm. When Pete asked him where he intended to go, Donald admitted that he had no plan. His car had been repossessed just before he left the city, and he was flat broke.

"I guess you'll have to stay with us," Pete said.

Donald put up a show of resistance. Then he gave in. "Just until I get my feet on the ground," he said.

"Right," Pete said. "Check out your options." He told Donald he'd send him money for a bus ticket, but as they were about to hang up Pete changed his mind. He knew that Donald would try hitchhiking to save the fare. Pete didn't want him out on the road all alone where some head case could pick him up, where anything could happen to him.

"Better yet," he said, "I'll come and get you."

"You don't have to do that. I didn't expect you to do that," Donald said. He added, "It's a pretty long drive."

"Just tell me how to get there."

But Donald wouldn't give him directions. He said that

the farm was too depressing, that Pete wouldn't like it. Instead, he insisted on meeting Pete at a service station called Jonathan's Mechanical Emporium.

"You must be kidding," Pete said.

"It's close to the highway," Donald said. "I didn't name it."

"That's one for the collection," Pete said.

The day before he left to bring Donald home, Pete received a letter from a man who described himself as "head of household" at the farm where Donald had been living. From this letter Pete learned that Donald had not quit the farm, but had been asked to leave. The letter was written on the back of a mimeographed survey form asking people to record their response to a ceremony of some kind. The last question said:

> *What did you feel during the liturgy?*
> a) *Being*
> b) *Becoming*
> c) *Being and Becoming*
> d) *None of the Above*
> e) *All of the Above*

Pete tried to forget the letter. But of course he couldn't. Each time he thought of it he felt crowded and breathless, a feeling that came over him again when he drove into the service station and saw Donald sitting against a wall with his head on his knees. It was late afternoon. A paper cup tumbled slowly past Donald's feet, pushed by the damp wind.

Pete honked and Donald raised his head. He smiled at

Pete, then stood and stretched. His arms were long and thin and white. He wore a red bandanna across his forehead, a T-shirt with a couple of words on the front. Pete couldn't read them because the letters were inverted.

"Grow up," Pete yelled. "Get a Mercedes."

Donald came up to the window. He bent down and said, "Thanks for coming. You must be totally whipped."

"I'll make it." Pete pointed at Donald's T-shirt. "What's that supposed to say?"

Donald looked down at his shirt front. "Try God. I guess I put it on backwards. Pete, could I borrow a couple of dollars? I owe these people for coffee and sandwiches."

Pete took five twenties from his wallet and held them out the window.

Donald stepped back as if horrified. "I don't need that much."

"I can't keep track of all these nickels and dimes," Pete said. "Just pay me back when your ship comes in." He waved the bills impatiently. "Go on — take it."

"Only for now." Donald took the money and went into the service station office. He came out carrying two orange sodas, one of which he gave to Pete as he got into the car. "My treat," he said.

"No bags?"

"Wow, thanks for reminding me," Donald said. He balanced his drink on the dashboard, but the slight rocking of the car as he got out tipped it onto the passenger's seat, where half its contents foamed over before Pete could snatch it up again. Donald looked on while Pete held the bottle out the window, soda running down his fingers.

"Wipe it up," Pete told him. "Quick!"

"With what?"

Pete stared at Donald. "That shirt. Use the shirt."

Donald pulled a long face but did as he was told, his pale skin puckering against the wind.

"Great, just great," Pete said. "We haven't even left the gas station yet."

Afterwards, on the highway, Donald said, "This is a new car, isn't it?"

"Yes. This is a new car."

"Is that why you're so upset about the seat?"

"Forget it, okay? Let's just forget about it."

"I said I was sorry."

Pete said, "I just wish you'd be more careful. These seats are made of leather. That stain won't come out, not to mention the smell. I don't see why I can't have leather seats that smell like leather instead of orange pop."

"What was wrong with the other car?"

Pete glanced over at Donald. Donald had raised the hood of the blue sweatshirt he'd put on. The peaked hood above his gaunt, watchful face gave him the look of an inquisitor.

"There wasn't anything wrong with it," Pete said. "I just happened to like this one better."

Donald nodded.

There was a long silence between them as Pete drove on and the day darkened toward evening. On either side of the road lay stubble-covered fields. A line of low hills ran along the horizon, topped here and there with trees black against the grey sky. In the approaching line of cars a driver turned on his headlights. Pete did the same.

"So what happened?" he asked. "Farm life not your bag?"

Donald took some time to answer, and at last he said, simply, "It was my fault."

"What was your fault?"

"The whole thing. Don't play dumb, Pete. I know they wrote to you." Donald looked at Pete, then stared out the windshield again.

"I'm not playing dumb."

Donald shrugged.

"All I really know is they asked you to leave," Pete went on. "I don't know any of the particulars."

"I blew it," Donald said. "Believe me, you don't want to hear the gory details."

"Sure I do," Pete said. He added, "Everybody likes the gory details."

"You mean everybody likes to hear how someone else messed up."

"Right," Pete said. "That's the way it is here on Spaceship Earth."

Donald bent one knee onto the front seat and leaned against the door so that he was facing Pete instead of the windshield. Pete was aware of Donald's scrutiny. He waited. Night was coming on in a rush now, filling the hollows of the land. Donald's long cheeks and deep-set eyes were dark with shadow. His brow was white. "Do you ever dream about me?" Donald asked.

"Do I ever dream about you? What kind of a question is that? Of course I don't dream about you," Pete said, untruthfully.

"What do you dream about?"

"Sex and money. Mostly money. A nightmare is when I dream I don't have any."

"You're just making that up," Donald said.

Pete smiled.

"Sometimes I wake up at night," Donald went on, "and I can tell you're dreaming about me."

"We were talking about the farm," Pete said. "Let's finish that conversation and then we can talk about our various out-of-body experiences and the interesting things we did during previous incarnations."

For a moment Donald looked like a grinning skull; then he turned serious again. "There's not that much to tell," he said. "I just didn't do anything right."

"That's a little vague," Pete said.

"Well, like the groceries. Whenever it was my turn to get the groceries I'd blow it somehow. I'd bring the groceries home and half of them would be missing, or I'd have all the wrong things, the wrong kind of flour or the wrong kind of chocolate or whatever. One time I gave them away. It's not funny, Pete."

Pete said, "Who did you give the groceries to?"

"Just some people I picked up on the way home. Some fieldworkers. They had about eight kids with them and they didn't even speak English — just nodded their heads. Still, I shouldn't have given away the groceries. Not all of them, anyway. I really learned my lesson about that. You have to be practical. You have to be fair to yourself." Donald leaned forward, and Pete could sense his excitement. "There's nothing actually wrong with being in business," he said. "As long as you're fair to other people you can still be fair to yourself. I'm thinking of going into business, Pete."

"We'll talk about it," Pete said. "So, that's the story? There isn't any more to it than that?"

"What did they tell you?" Donald asked.

"Nothing."

"They must have told you something."

Pete shook his head.

"They didn't tell you about the fire?" When Pete shook his head again Donald regarded him for a time, then said, "I don't know. It was stupid. I just completely lost it." He folded his arms across his chest and slumped back into the corner. "Everybody had to take turns cooking dinner. I usually did tuna casserole or spaghetti with garlic bread. But this one night I thought I'd do something different, something really interesting." Donald looked sharply at Pete. "It's all a big laugh to you, isn't it?"

"I'm sorry," Pete said.

"You don't know when to quit. You just keep hitting away."

"Tell me about the fire, Donald."

Donald kept watching him. "You have this compulsion to make me look foolish."

"Come off it, Donald. Don't make a big thing out of this."

"I know why you do it. It's because you don't have any purpose in life. You're afraid to relate to people who do, so you make fun of them."

"Relate," Pete said softly.

"You're basically a very frightened individual," Donald said. "Very threatened. You've always been like that. Do you remember when you used to try to kill me?"

"I don't have any compulsion to make you look foolish, Donald — you do it yourself. You're doing it right now."

"You can't tell me you don't remember," Donald said. "It was after my operation. You remember that."

"Sort of." Pete shrugged. "Not really."

"Oh yes," Donald said. "Do you want to see the scar?"

"I remember you had an operation. I don't remember

the specifics, that's all. And I sure as hell don't remember trying to kill you."

"Oh yes," Donald repeated, maddeningly. "You bet your life you did. All the time. The thing was, I couldn't have anything happen to me where they sewed me up because then my intestines would come apart again and poison me. That was a big issue, Pete. Mom was always in a state about me climbing trees and so on. And you used to hit me there every chance you got."

"Mom was in a state every time you burped," Pete said. "I don't know. Maybe I bumped into you accidentally once or twice. I never did it deliberately."

"Every chance you got," Donald said. "Like when the folks went out at night and left you to baby-sit. I'd hear them say good night, and then I'd hear the car start up, and when they were gone I'd lie there and listen. After a while I would hear you coming down the hall, and I would close my eyes and pretend to be asleep. There were nights when you would stand outside the door, just stand there, and then go away again. But most nights you'd open the door and I would hear you in the room with me, breathing. You'd come over and sit next to me on the bed — you remember, Pete, you have to — you'd sit next to me on the bed and pull the sheets back. If I was on my stomach you'd roll me over. Then you would lift up my pajama shirt and start hitting me on my stitches. You'd hit me as hard as you could, over and over. And I would just keep lying there with my eyes closed. I was afraid that you'd get mad if you knew I was awake. Is that strange or what? I was afraid that you'd get mad if you found out that I knew you were trying to kill me." Donald laughed. "Come on, you can't tell me you don't remember that."

"It might have happened once or twice. Kids do those

things. I can't get all excited about something I maybe did twenty-five years ago."

"No maybe about it. You did it."

Pete said, "You're wearing me out with this stuff. We've got a long drive ahead of us and if you don't back off pretty soon we aren't going to make it. You aren't, anyway."

Donald turned away.

"I'm doing my best," Pete said. The self-pity in his own voice made the words sound like a lie. But they weren't a lie! He was doing his best.

The car topped a rise. In the distance Pete saw a cluster of lights that blinked out when he started downhill. There was no moon. The sky was low and black.

"Come to think of it," Pete said, "I did have a dream about you the other night." Then he added, impatiently, as if Donald were badgering him, "A couple of other nights too. I'm getting hungry," he said.

"The same dream?"

"Different dreams. I only remember one of them well. There was something wrong with me, and you were helping out. Taking care of me. Just the two of us. I don't know where everyone else was supposed to be."

Pete left it at that. He didn't tell Donald that in this dream he was blind.

"I wonder if that was when I woke up," Donald said. He added, "I'm sorry I got into that thing about my scar. I keep trying to forget it but I guess I never will. Not really. It was pretty strange, having someone around all the time who wanted to get rid of me."

"Kid stuff," Pete said. "Ancient history."

. . .

They ate dinner at a Denny's on the other side of King City. As Pete was paying the check he heard a man behind him say, "Excuse me, but I wonder if I might ask which way you're going?" and Donald answer, "Santa Cruz."

"Perfect," the man said.

Pete could see him in the fish-eye mirror above the cash register: a red blazer with some kind of crest on the pocket, little black moustache, glossy black hair combed down on his forehead like a Roman emperor's. A rug, Pete thought. Definitely a rug.

Pete got his change and turned. "Why is that perfect?" he asked.

The man looked at Pete. He had a soft ruddy face that was doing its best to express pleasant surprise, as if this new wrinkle were all he could have wished for, but the eyes behind the aviator glasses showed signs of regret. His lips were moist and shiny. "I take it you're together," he said.

"You got it," Pete told him.

"All the better, then," the man went on. "It so happens I'm going to Santa Cruz myself. Had a spot of car trouble down the road. The old Caddy let me down."

"What kind of trouble?" Pete asked.

"Engine trouble," the man said. "I'm afraid it's a bit urgent. My daughter is sick. Urgently sick. I've got a telegram here." He patted the breast pocket of his blazer.

Pete grinned. Amazing, he thought, the old sick daughter ploy, but before he could say anything Donald got into the act again. "No problem," Donald said. "We've got tons of room."

"Not that much room," Pete said.

Donald nodded. "I'll put my things in the trunk."

"The trunk's full," Pete told him.

"It so happens I'm traveling light," the man said. "This leg of the trip anyway. In fact I don't have any luggage at this particular time."

Pete said, "Left it in the old Caddy, did you?"

"Exactly," the man said.

"No problem," Donald repeated. He walked outside and the man went with him. Together they strolled across the parking lot, Pete following at a distance. When they reached Pete's car Donald raised his face to the sky, and the man did the same. They stood there looking up. "Dark night," Donald said.

"Stygian," the man said.

Pete still had it in mind to brush him off, but he didn't do that. Instead he unlocked the door for him. He wanted to see what would happen. It was an adventure, but not a dangerous adventure. The man might steal Pete's ashtrays but he wouldn't kill him. If Pete got killed on the road it would be by some spiritual person in a sweatsuit, someone with his eyes on the far horizon and a wet Try God T-shirt in his duffel bag.

As soon as they left the parking lot the man lit a cigar. He blew a cloud of smoke over Pete's shoulder and sighed with pleasure. "Put it out," Pete told him.

"Of course," the man said. Pete looked into the rear-view mirror and saw the man take another long puff before dropping the cigar out the window. "Forgive me," he said. "I should have asked. Name's Webster, by the way."

Donald turned and looked back at him. "First name or last?"

The man hesitated. "Last," he said finally.

"I know a Webster," Donald said. "Mick Webster."

"There are many of us," Webster said.

"Big fellow, wooden leg," Pete said.

Donald gave Pete a look.

Webster shook his head. "Doesn't ring a bell. Still, I wouldn't deny the connection. Might be one of the cousinry."

"What's your daughter got?" Pete asked.

"That isn't clear," Webster answered. "It appears to be a female complaint of some nature. Then again it may be tropical." He was quiet for a moment, and added: "If indeed it *is* tropical, I will have to assume some of the blame myself. It was my own vaulting ambition that first led us to the tropics and kept us in the tropics all those many years, exposed to every evil. Truly I have much to answer for. I left my wife there."

Donald said quietly, "You mean she died?"

"I buried her with these hands. The earth will be repaid, gold for gold."

"Which tropics?" Pete asked.

"The tropics of Peru."

"What part of Peru are they in?"

"The lowlands," Webster said.

Pete nodded. "What's it like down there?"

"Another world," Webster said. His tone was sepulchral. "A world better imagined than described."

"Far out," Pete said.

The three men rode in silence for a time. A line of trucks went past in the other direction, trailers festooned with running lights, engines roaring.

"Yes," Webster said at last, "I have much to answer for."

Pete smiled at Donald, but Donald had turned in his seat again and was gazing at Webster. "I'm sorry about your wife," Donald said.

"What did she die of?" Pete asked.

"A wasting illness," Webster said. "The doctors have no name for it, but I do." He leaned forward and said, fiercely, "*Greed.*" Then he slumped back against his seat. "My greed, not hers. She wanted no part of it."

Pete bit his lip. Webster was a find and Pete didn't want to scare him off by hooting at him. In a voice low and innocent of knowingness, he asked, "What took you there?"

"It's difficult for me to talk about."

"Try," Pete told him.

"A cigar would make it easier."

Donald turned to Pete and said, "It's okay with me."

"All right," Pete said. "Go ahead. Just keep the window rolled down."

"Much obliged." A match flared. There were eager sucking sounds.

"Let's hear it," Pete said.

"I am by training an engineer," Webster began. "My work has exposed me to all but one of the continents, to desert and alp and forest, to every terrain and season of the earth. Some years ago I was hired by the Peruvian government to search for tungsten in the tropics. My wife and daughter accompanied me. We were the only white people for a thousand miles in any direction, and we had no choice but to live as the Indians lived — to share their food and drink and even their culture."

Pete said, "You knew the lingo, did you?"

"We picked it up." The ember of the cigar bobbed up and down. "We were used to learning as necessity decreed. At any rate, it became evident after a couple of years that there was no tungsten to be found. My wife had fallen ill and was pleading to be taken home. But I was deaf to her pleas, because by then I was on the trail of another metal — a metal far more valuable than tungsten."

"Let me guess," Pete said. "Gold?"

Donald looked at Pete, then back at Webster.

"Gold," Webster said. "A vein of gold greater than the Mother Lode itself. After I found the first traces of it nothing could tear me away from my search — not the sickness of my wife nor anything else. I was determined to uncover the vein, and so I did — but not before I laid my wife to rest. As I say, the earth will be repaid."

Webster was quiet. Then he said, "But life must go on. In the years since my wife's death I have been making the arrangements necessary to open the mine. I could have done it immediately, of course, enriching myself beyond measure, but I knew what that would mean — the exploitation of our beloved Indians, the brutal destruction of their environment. I felt I had too much to atone for already." Webster paused, and when he spoke again his voice was dull and rushed, as if he had used up all the interest he had in his own words. "Instead I drew up a program for returning the bulk of the wealth to the Indians themselves. A kind of trust fund. The interest alone will allow them to secure their ancient lands and rights in perpetuity. At the same time, our investors will be rewarded a thousandfold. Two-thousandfold. Everyone will prosper together."

"That's great," Donald said. "That's the way it ought to be."

Pete said, "I'm willing to bet that you just happen to have a few shares left. Am I right?"

Webster made no reply.

"Well?" Pete knew that Webster was on to him now, but

he didn't care. The story had bored him. He'd expected something different, something original, and Webster had let him down. He hadn't even tried. Pete felt sour and stale. His eyes burned from cigar smoke and the high beams of road-hogging truckers. "Douse the stogie," he said to Webster. "I told you to keep the window down."

"Got a little nippy back here."

Donald said, "Hey, Pete. Lighten up."

"Douse it!"

Webster sighed. He got rid of the cigar.

"I'm a wreck," Pete said to Donald. "You want to drive for a while?"

Donald nodded.

Pete pulled over and they changed places.

Webster kept his counsel in the back seat. Donald hummed while he drove, until Pete told him to stop. Then everything was quiet.

Donald was humming again when Pete woke up. Pete stared sullenly at the road, at the white lines sliding past the car. After a few moments of this he turned and said, "How long have I been out?"

Donald glanced at him. "Twenty, twenty-five minutes."

Pete looked behind him and saw that Webster was gone. "Where's our friend?"

"You just missed him. He got out in Soledad. He told me to say thanks and good-bye."

"Soledad? What about his sick daughter? How did he explain her away?" Pete leaned over the seat. Both ashtrays were still in place. Floor mats. Door handles.

"He has a brother living there. He's going to borrow a car from him and drive the rest of the way in the morning."

"I'll bet his brother's living there," Pete said. "Doing fifty concurrent life sentences. His brother and his sister and his mom and his dad."

"I kind of liked him," Donald said.

"I'm sure you did," Pete said wearily.

"He was interesting. He'd been places."

"His cigars had been places, I'll give you that."

"Come on, Pete."

"Come on yourself. What a phony."

"You don't know that."

"Sure I do."

"How? How do you know?"

Pete stretched. "Brother, there are some things you're just born knowing. What's the gas situation?"

"We're a little low."

"Then why didn't you get some more?"

"I wish you wouldn't snap at me like that," Donald said.

"Then why don't you use your head? What if we run out?"

"We'll make it," Donald said. "I'm pretty sure we've got enough to make it. You didn't have to be so rude to him," Donald added.

Pete took a deep breath. "I don't feel like running out of gas tonight, okay?"

Donald pulled in at the next station they came to and filled the tank while Pete went to the men's room. When Pete came back, Donald was sitting in the passenger's seat. The attendant came up to the driver's window as Pete got in behind the wheel. He bent down and said, "Twelve fifty-five."

"You heard the man," Pete said to Donald.

Donald looked straight ahead. He didn't move.

"Cough up," Pete said. "This trip's on you."

Donald said, softly, "I can't."

"Sure you can. Break out that wad."

Donald glanced up at the attendant, then at Pete. "Please," he said. "Pete, I don't have it anymore."

Pete took this in. He nodded, and paid the attendant.

Donald began to speak when they left the station but Pete cut him off. He said, "I don't want to hear from you right now. You just keep quiet or I swear to God I won't be responsible."

They left the fields and entered a tunnel of tall trees. The trees went on and on. "Let me get this straight," Pete said at last. "You don't have the money I gave you."

"You treated him like a bug or something," Donald said.

"You don't have the money," Pete said again.

Donald shook his head.

"Since I bought dinner, and since we didn't stop anywhere in between, I assume you gave it to Webster. Is that right? Is that what you did with it?"

"Yes."

Pete looked at Donald. His face was dark under the hood but he still managed to convey a sense of remove, as if none of this had anything to do with him.

"Why?" Pete asked. "Why did you give it to him?" When Donald didn't answer, Pete said, "A hundred dollars. Gone. Just like that. I *worked* for that money, Donald."

"I know, I know," Donald said.

"You don't know! How could you? You get money by holding out your hand."

"I work too," Donald said.

"You work too. Don't kid yourself, brother."

Donald leaned toward Pete, about to say something, but Pete cut him off again.

"You're not the only one on the payroll, Donald. I don't think you understand that. I have a family."

"Pete, I'll pay you back."

"Like hell you will. A hundred dollars!" Pete hit the steering wheel with the palm of his hand. "Just because you think I hurt some goofball's feelings. Jesus, Donald."

"That's not the reason," Donald said. "And I didn't just *give* him the money."

"What do you call it, then? What do you call what you did?"

"I *invested* it. I wanted a share, Pete." When Pete looked over at him Donald nodded and said again, "I wanted a share."

Pete said, "I take it you're referring to the gold mine in Peru."

"Yes," Donald said.

"You believe that such a gold mine exists?"

Donald looked at Pete, and Pete could see him just beginning to catch on. "You'll believe anything," Pete said. "Won't you? You really will believe anything at all."

"I'm sorry," Donald said, and turned away.

Pete drove on between the trees and considered the truth of what he had just said — that Donald would believe anything at all. And it came to him that it would be just like this unfair life for Donald to come out ahead in the end, by believing in some outrageous promise that would turn out to be true and that he, Pete, would reject out of hand because he was too wised up to listen to anybody's pitch anymore except for laughs. What a joke. What a joke if there really was a blessing to be had, and the blessing didn't come to the one who deserved it, the one who did all the work, but to the other.

And as if this had already happened Pete felt a shadow move upon him, darkening his thoughts. After a time he said, "I can see where all this is going, Donald."

"I'll pay you back," Donald said.

"No," Pete said. "You won't pay me back. You can't. You don't know how. All you've ever done is take. All your life."

Donald shook his head.

"I see exactly where this is going," Pete went on. "You can't work, you can't take care of yourself, you believe anything anyone tells you. I'm stuck with you, aren't I?" He looked over at Donald. "I've got you on my hands for good."

Donald pressed his fingers against the dashboard as if to brace himself. "I'll get out," he said.

Pete kept driving.

"Let me out," Donald said. "I mean it, Pete."

"Do you?"

Donald hesitated. "Yes," he said.

"Be sure," Pete told him. "This is it. This is for keeps."

"I mean it."

"All right. You made the choice." Pete braked the car sharply and swung it to the shoulder of the road. He turned off the engine and got out. Trees loomed on both sides, shutting out the sky. The air was cold and musty. Pete took Donald's duffel bag from the back seat and set it down behind the car. He stood there, facing Donald in the red glow of the taillights. "It's better this way," Pete said.

Donald just looked at him.

"Better for you," Pete said.

Donald hugged himself. He was shaking. "You don't have to say all that," he told Pete. "I don't blame you."

"Blame me? What the hell are you talking about? Blame me for what?"

"For anything," Donald said.

"I want to know what you mean by blame me."

"Nothing. Nothing, Pete. You'd better get going. God bless you."

"That's it," Pete said. He dropped to one knee, searching the packed dirt with his hands. He didn't know what he was looking for; his hands would know when they found it.

Donald touched Pete's shoulder. "You'd better go," he said.

Somewhere in the trees Pete heard a branch snap. He stood up. He looked at Donald, then went back to the car and drove away. He drove fast, hunched over the wheel, conscious of the way he was hunched and the shallowness of his breathing, refusing to look at the mirror above his head until there was nothing behind him but darkness.

Then he said, "A hundred dollars," as if there were someone to hear.

The trees gave way to fields. Metal fences ran beside the road, plastered with windblown scraps of paper. Tule fog hung above the ditches, spilling into the road, dimming the ghostly halogen lights that burned in the yards of the farms Pete passed. The fog left beads of water rolling up the windshield.

Pete rummaged among his cassettes. He found Pachelbel's Canon and pushed it into the tape deck. When the

violins began to play he leaned back and assumed an atten-
tive expression as if he were really listening to them. He
smiled to himself like a man at liberty to enjoy music, a
man who has finished his work and settled his debts, done
all things meet and due.

And in this way, smiling, nodding to the music, he went
another mile or so and pretended that he was not already
slowing down, that he was not going to turn back, that he
would be able to drive on like this, alone, and have the
right answer when his wife stood before him in the doorway of his home and asked, Where is he? Where is
your brother?

TOBIAS WOLFF grew up in the Pacific North-
west, where many of his stories are set. His fiction
appears frequently in *The Atlantic, Esquire, Vanity Fair, Antaeus, TriQuarterly,* and other magazines in this country and abroad. Mr. Wolff has
received numerous honors and awards, including
the PEN/Faulkner Award for his short novel *The
Barracks Thief.* He lives with his wife, Catherine,
and their two sons in upstate New York
and teaches at Syracuse University.